Praise for the Gods and Warriors series

The Outsiders

'. . . the reader is instantly plunged into danger and excitement . . . A deft, suspenseful story . . .' *The Times*

'Paver's immaculate research, control of pace, intricate plotting and fully formed characters build an excellent adventure . . . A guaranteed bestseller' *Daily Mail*

'My ten year old was totally gripped. The book of the autumn' *Angels and Urchins*

'The reader's attention is caught from the first line . . . the book has a spellbinding storyline' Oscar, aged 13, *Daily Telegraph*

'To spend an hour with Michelle Paver is to lose yourself in another place and time . . . Appealing to both girls and boys, *Gods and Warriors* looks set to become another children's classic' *****
Books for Keeps

'This is an exceptional read for eight to ten-year-olds'
Telegraph Weekend

'. . . exciting, interesting and, well, just super. The characters move forwards and the animal character is wonderful. And of course, it's beautifully researched'
The Bookbag

'Hats off to another rollicking adventure story with some sound educational side-effects to boot'
Independent

The Eye of the Falcon

'You get a satisfying adventure, characters to root for, animals to fall in love with, and a vivid picture of a world long gone. Honestly, what more could you want?'
The Bookbag

'Michelle Paver has a real gift for writing about animals and she writes brilliantly about Havoc the lion cub'
Parents in Touch

Books by Michelle Paver

Gods and Warriors:

The Outsiders

The Burning Shadow

The Eye of the Falcon

The Crocodile Tomb

Chronicles of Ancient Darkness:

Wolf Brother

Spirit Walker

Soul Eater

Outcast

Oath Breaker

Ghost Hunter

For older readers

Dark Matter

GODS AND WARRIORS

THE CROCODILE TOMB

MICHELLE PAVER

PUFFIN

PUFFIN BOOKS

UK | USA | Canada | Ireland | Australia
India | New Zealand | South Africa

Puffin Books is part of the Penguin Random House group of companies
whose addresses can be found at global.penguinrandomhouse.com.

puffinbooks.com

First published 2015
001

Text copyright © Michelle Paver, 2015
Map, logo and illustrations copyright © Puffin Books, 2015
Map and illustrations by Fred Van Deelen
Logo design by James Fraser
The moral right of the author and illustrator has been asserted

Set in 13/18 pt Dante MT Std
Typeset by Jouve (UK), Milton Keynes
Printed in Great Britain by Clays Ltd, St Ives plc

A CIP catalogue record for this book is available from the British Library

ISBN: 978-0-141-33933-7

www.greenpenguin.co.uk

THE WORLD OF GODS AND WARRIORS

PROLOGUE

The leopard lay on the floor with its eyes shut and its thick tail curled around one leg of the ebony chair. The monkey crouched above it on the roofbeam, torn between terror of the sleeping monster and desire for the green glass bowl on the table, which was heaped with pomegranates, figs and dates.

Nervously baring its teeth, the monkey stretched out one scrawny arm, but couldn't reach the fruit. The monkey drew back, champing its teeth in frustration. The leopard twisted one ear to catch the sound, and went on pretending to be asleep. The monkey didn't notice. All it saw was the fruit.

This time, the monkey gripped the roofbeam with one foot and swung down with both arms extended – and the huge cat struck. A blur of black and gold, a shriek, a crunch – and it was over.

Alekto laughed and clapped her hennaed hands. 'But it didn't last *long* enough!' she complained to the fat Egyptian nobleman seated beside her. 'It hardly suffered at all! Can we find another one?'

She looked extremely beautiful and very un-Egyptian in her spiked gold diadem and her tight-waisted robe of yellow silk, and Kerasher bowed low. 'Anything, my lady,' he said in heavily accented Akean.

'My Lord Kerasher, we have no time,' snapped Telamon as he paced up and down. 'You said they're bringing the prisoner?'

The Egyptian inclined his head in assent, and Alekto gave Telamon a mocking bow. 'How *masterful* you are, nephew!'

Telamon glared at her. She was only a few years older than him, but she loved calling him 'nephew', as it made him sound like a boy. 'This prisoner,' he said to Kerasher. 'You're sure it's him?'

'So my men tell me,' said the Egyptian, with slightly forced politeness. 'But only you, my Lord Telamon, know the face of the man you seek, so it will be for you to say.'

Telamon went on pacing. 'When?'

'Soon.'

'It's always "soon",' muttered Telamon.

He *hated* Egypt. The heat, the swampy River, this fat brown man with his jewelled collar and his green eye-paint that was starting to run in the heat. Kerasher had been sent by the Perao Himself, the god-king of Egypt, to help them find the dagger, but Telamon could feel the disdain behind his smiles. What made it worse was that the Egyptian was so horribly *womanish*, with his elaborate plaited wig and his painted, beardless face. He even had his slaves shave the hair off his *legs*.

It's Hylas' fault that I'm here, Telamon thought savagely. Hylas and Pirra together. If they hadn't stolen the dagger – if Pirra's slave hadn't brought it to Egypt . . .

Alekto snapped her fingers at her new plaything. The leopard left its kill, padded over to her, and laid its blood-stained head on her knees. 'What else can we feed it?' she murmured. 'And this time, Lord Kerasher, make it *last*!' Bending her lovely head to the beast's bloody muzzle, she put out her little pointed tongue and licked it.

Kerasher's eyes were glazed and his mouth was hanging open. Practically dribbling with lust, thought Telamon in disgust.

Alekto caught his eye and grinned. He didn't grin

back. He hated her, too. She was always laughing at him and belittling him in front of his warriors. For the hundredth time, he wished his uncle Pharax had been with him, instead of her.

But then, he reminded himself, it would be Pharax in command of this mission, not you. And you *are* in command, Telamon, whatever Alekto might think. You are the grandson of Koronos, High Chieftain of Mycenae. He sent *you* to Egypt because he knows you will succeed.

Footsteps outside, and a clink of armour.

The leopard twitched its tail, and Alekto gripped the arms of her chair.

'At last,' said Telamon.

They'd flung the prisoner face down at Telamon's feet: a young man in a dusty kilt with his arms pinioned painfully behind his back. One of the guards yanked him into a kneeling position, and Telamon caught his breath. 'It's him! Did he have it? Did they find the dagger?'

'He had this,' said Kerasher. Another guard held out a knife with a cheap bone hilt and a copper blade.

With a snarl, Telamon flung it aside. 'That's not it!'

Kerasher permitted himself a small sigh. 'Then I will question him –'

'No,' cut in Telamon. 'I'll do it, he speaks Akean.' Then to the prisoner, 'Where's the dagger?'

No reply. The prisoner was watching the leopard tearing at the monkey's blue guts.

'Look at me!' barked Telamon. 'Where is the dagger of Koronos?'

Like many Egyptians, the prisoner had a shaven head and black-rimmed eyes. It was a handsome face, striving for blankness. The dark gaze met Telamon's and he shook his head.

'He knows where it is,' said Alekto, watching the prisoner with the fixity of a snake with its prey.

'I will have him beaten like a strip of papyrus,' said Kerasher. 'If he does not tell . . .' One fat bejewelled hand indicated his men's crescent-moon axes and copper-tipped whips.

Alekto drew back her lips from her teeth and gave a little shiver of excitement. 'Oh, I think we can do better than that.'

For the first time since they'd left Mycenae, Telamon was glad she was with him. He disliked torture, but Alekto *loved* it. She would make the prisoner talk.

Soon they would have the dagger. Telamon's heart

quickened as he remembered the long vicious sweep of its blade, and the feel of his ancestors' strength surging through him as he gripped the hilt . . .

'Let's make a start,' said Alekto. Her cheeks were flushed, her beautiful lips parted.

'Not yet,' Telamon said coldly. Squatting on his heels, he showed the prisoner the little amethyst falcon on his wrist. The slave's face twisted with pain and grief. The sealstone had belonged to Pirra.

'Userref,' Telamon said quietly. 'Tell me where you hid the dagger and I'll give you a painless death. Your people will bury you with the proper rites and your spirit will join your ancestors. But refuse – and we will *make* you tell. Then we will fling your body to the crows and your spirit will be lost for ever. So. Take the easy way.'

Again Userref's eyes met his. Again he shook his head. Telamon was surprised that a mere slave could be so brave.

Behind him, Kerasher stirred. 'Let us take him back to –'

'No,' said Telamon. 'We've wasted enough time.' Rising to his feet, he glanced at Alekto. He was gratified to see that she was waiting for him to give the word. He *was* in command. The gods *were* with him. Soon the dagger of Koronos would be his – and this time, neither Hylas nor Pirra could stop him, for they were far away in Keftiu. Nothing could stop him now.

Putting his hands on his hips, he squared his shoulders. 'Let's get started,' he said.

I

'This is like no land I've ever seen,' muttered Hylas. 'There's nothing here.' Only the Sea lying stunned beneath the Sun, and this vast shimmering plain of endless red sand.

'It's nothing like Egypt, either,' said Pirra. 'Userref said Egypt's got a huge river down the middle, and fields and villages and temples along the banks. He said . . .' She licked her lips. 'He said that on either side of it there's only endless red sand. He called it – *deshret*.'

'Desert,' said Hylas.

She met his eyes. 'It's where they bury their dead.'

Deshret.

The Sun was fiercer than he'd ever known, the air so hot it was like breathing smoke. Squinting in the glare, he scanned the quivering plain. No villages, no river. Just the odd clump of rocks and dusty scrub, and a twist of windblown sand whirling like a demon over the ground.

Far out on the Sea, their ship had dwindled to a speck. 'They never intended to take us to Egypt,' he said bitterly. 'They stole our gold and dumped us here to die.'

'They could've killed us and chucked us overboard,' Pirra pointed out. 'And they did leave us our weapons.'

'What, so we're *lucky*?'

'No, but we're alive.'

She was right – but he wanted to rage and fling curses at those filthy, lying Phoenicians. For over a moon, he and Pirra had hidden in the Keftian hills with Echo and Havoc, desperately waiting for a ship bound for Egypt. When at last they'd found one willing to take them, it had been blown off course, and the crew had blamed *them*. 'Foreigners bring bad luck,' the captain had declared. And who could be more outlandish than an Akean boy with strange tawny hair and a young lioness at his side, and a Keftian girl with a crescent-moon scar on her cheek and a falcon on her wrist?

Havoc padded past Hylas, then glanced back at him

for reassurance. She still behaved like a cub, as if she hadn't yet realized that she was nearly full-grown. After days of sea sickness, she was gaunt and bedraggled, and now besieged by flies. She stood panting, miserably twitching her ears.

Hylas untied the neck of the waterskin and poured a little into his cupped hand, and she slurped it up with a rasping lick that nearly took the skin off his palm. 'Sorry I can't give you more,' he told her. The waterskin was only half full. It wouldn't last long.

'Maybe Egypt's not far away,' said Pirra. 'Rivers flow into the Sea, don't they? If we walk along the coast, we might find it.'

'Unless we go the wrong way and end up heading deeper into the desert.'

Echo, soaring overhead, suddenly wheeled off across the plain. 'Maybe she knows where it is,' said Pirra, watching the falcon fly.

Hylas didn't reply. Echo could fly for days without water. They couldn't. He could see Pirra thinking the same thing. 'Come on,' he said. 'Let's dig a hole, see if we can find anything to drink.'

A searing wind flung grit in his eyes as they trudged up the shore. Sweat trickled down his back, soaking the coil of rope slung across his shoulder. He felt the ground burning through the soles of his rawhide sandals. Around him the heat danced, so that his shadow seemed to be moving on its own. There was a throbbing pain in his skull. He prayed that was only the glare, and not the ache he always got before a vision.

Fifty paces in from the Sea, they knelt and started digging with their hands. They dug as far as they could. Soon, moisture seeped into the bottom of the hole. Hylas tasted it – and spat it out. 'Salt,' he said in disgust.

Pirra cast about her. 'Berries on that bush over there. Can we eat them?'

Hylas blinked. He was an Outsider who'd grown up in the wild, he knew every plant in Akea. But he'd never seen this one. 'I don't know,' he said uneasily. 'We can't risk it, it might be poisonous.'

Havoc padded over to the bush and slumped down in its pitiful strip of shade, batting at the flies with her forepaws.

The bush gave an angry hiss.

Havoc scrambled to her feet and backed away.

Before Hylas or Pirra could take in what was happening, a snake shot out from under the bush. But instead of slithering off, it turned and rose up on the end of its tail – it swayed its flat black head from side to side, and *spat* at Havoc. She dodged. The jet of venom missed her eye and hit her nose instead. Hylas threw his knife. It struck just behind the head, pinning the snake to the sand. As it twisted and thrashed, Pirra finished it off with a rock.

A shaken silence.

Havoc sneezed and rubbed her muzzle in the sand. Hylas retrieved his knife and hacked off the head.

'Have you ever seen a snake do that?' panted Pirra.

'No,' he said curtly.

They exchanged glances. Killing the first creature they met had to be a bad omen. And for all they knew, this snake was sacred to whatever strange gods ruled this land.

Havoc was patting the carcass with a curious forepaw. Hylas pushed her aside and wiped the last of the venom off her nose with the hem of his tunic.

'D'you think we can eat it?' said Pirra.

'I don't know,' he muttered. Anger tightened his throat. 'I don't *know*!' he cried, lashing out at the bush with his knife. 'I don't *know* these plants or these creatures! I don't *know* if we can eat these berries, and I've never seen a snake stand on its tail and spit!'

'Hylas, stop it, you're frightening Havoc!'

The young lioness had retreated behind Pirra's legs, and was staring at him with her ears back.

'Sorry,' he mumbled.

Havoc came over and rubbed her furry cheek against his thigh. He scratched her big golden head, as much to reassure himself as her.

'When I first met you,' Pirra said levelly, 'we were stuck on an island with no food and no water. But we survived.'

'That was different.'

'I know, but if anyone can survive out here, it's you.'

Echo swept down on to Pirra's shoulder and gave a lock of her dark hair an affectionate tug. Pirra touched the falcon's scaly yellow foot with one finger.

Havoc was gazing up at Hylas, her great golden eyes full of trust.

'Right,' he said. 'We've got half a skin of water, two knives, my slingshot, a coil of rope and a dead snake. *If* we can eat it.'

'Animals know if something's poisoned, don't they?' said Pirra. 'If Havoc and Echo think it's all right . . .'

Hylas nodded. 'Let's find out.' Cutting a chunk off the tail, he tossed it to Havoc, then gave a smaller piece to Pirra, who held it in her fist. Echo hopped on to the rawhide cuff Pirra wore on her forearm, ripped the meat to shreds and gulped it down. Havoc was already crunching hers messily to bits.

'Looks like it's all right,' said Pirra.

'And there might be fish in the Sea,' said Hylas.

She gave him a wry smile. 'And the Phoenicians didn't get *all* the gold, I hid a necklace under my tunic – so if we can find someone selling food, we'll be fine!'

He snorted a laugh.

It was nearly noon. The heat was unbearable.

'Havoc had the right idea,' he said. 'We've got to get out of this sun.'

Pirra pointed up the coast, where a rocky outcrop shimmered in the distance. 'Might be a cave among those rocks.'

'Let's go.'

Hylas felt a bit better. But as they started towards the rocks, he realized that finding Egypt, and Userref, and the dagger of Koronos, no longer mattered.

First, they had to stay alive.

2

They'd cut strips off their tunics and wet them in the Sea, then wound them round their heads. The sopping cloth had been wonderfully cool, but it soon dried, and now Pirra could feel the Sun hammering her skull. Her eyes were scratchy, her tongue was a lump of sand. She thought she kept hearing the trickle of water, but there wasn't any. Only the deathlike silence of the desert.

Hylas stumbled along beside her, squinting and rubbing his temples. She worried that he might be about to have a vision. What would he see? Ghosts? Demons? If it happened, he would tell her when he was ready, but she'd learnt not to ask. He hated talking about it. 'It's frightening and it hurts,' he'd said once. 'I never know when it's going to happen. I just wish it would stop.'

The outcrop of big red boulders wasn't getting any closer. She wondered if it was really there, or just a trick of the gods.

A trick of the gods . . .

She halted. 'Hylas, we're doing this all wrong.'

'What?' he croaked.

'Whatever gods rule this place, they won't help us till we've made an offering.'

Hylas looked at her, appalled. 'I can't believe I forgot.'

'Me too. We should've done it as soon as we got ashore. We won't make it if we don't.'

Hylas wiped the sweat off his face and tossed her the lion claw he wore on a thong around his neck, while she took off Userref's *wedjat* eye amulet, which she'd worn ever since Keftiu. Muttering a swift prayer under her breath, she found a clump of scrub and tucked the snake's head in its branches. It would be safe from Echo, who'd flown off to hunt; and Havoc was plodding ahead and hadn't noticed. After touching both amulets to the offering, Pirra stumbled back to Hylas and handed him his lion claw.

'Who did you offer to?' he said as they resumed their trudge.

'The Goddess for me, Lady of the Wild Things for you, and two of the most powerful gods of Egypt.'

'Who?' He was scanning the ground for pebbles for his slingshot.

'Heru – He has a falcon's head – and Sekhmet, She has the head of a lioness. I remembered them because of Echo and Havoc.'

Hylas slipped a pebble into the pouch at his belt. 'Are there more?'

'Lots. Userref used to tell me stories when I was little . . .' She broke off. Userref had looked after her since she was a baby, and she missed him terribly. For fourteen years he'd played with her and scolded her, tried to keep her out of trouble, and told her all about his beloved Egypt. He was far more than a slave. He was the big brother she'd never had.

'Pirra?' said Hylas. 'What are the other gods?'

'Um – there's one with the head of something called a jackal, I think that's a kind of fox. And one like a river horse –'

'A *what*?'

'They're very fat, with a huge snout, and they live in the river. Also there's a god like a crocodile, whatever that is.'

He frowned. 'When I was a slave down the mines, there was an Egyptian boy, he talked about crocodiles. He said they're giant lizards with hide tougher than armour, and they eat people. I thought he was making it up.'

'I'm pretty sure they're real.'

He didn't reply. He was squinting at the outcrop, which was now only forty paces away. 'Your eyes are better than mine. Can you see people clambering about?'

Pirra's heart leapt. Through the shimmering air, she glimpsed tiny dark figures moving among the rocks. 'The offering worked!' she croaked. 'We're saved!'

The nearer they got, the more uneasy Hylas became. Those people moved astonishingly fast – but they were scrambling about on all fours.

He grabbed Pirra's arm. 'Those aren't men!'

She shaded her eyes with her hand. 'What *are* they?' she whispered.

They looked like a cross between men and dogs: covered in dense greyish-brown fur, with thick tails, long powerful arms, and narrow bony red faces.

Hylas wondered if they were demons. But although he felt dizzy, and the rocks and even his shadow trembled in the heat, there was no burning finger stabbing his temple, as there always was when he had a vision.

Suddenly, he felt watched.

'*Look,*' breathed Pirra.

To their right, twenty paces from where they stood, one of the creatures crouched on top of a solitary boulder. It was bigger than the others; Hylas guessed it was the leader. He saw its massive chest matted with blood, its heavy brows overhanging small yellow eyes set very close together. Glaring at him.

'Don't run,' Hylas said quietly. 'Don't turn your back on it or it'll think we're prey.'

Slowly, they began to edge backwards.

The creature bared huge white fangs and uttered a harsh rattling bark. It sounded horribly like a signal.

Behind it, the other creatures had clustered at the base of the outcrop. They glanced up at their leader's barks, then went back to their kill. Hylas glimpsed the carcass of a large white buck with a long spiral horn. He saw strong man-like hands snapping its ribs, ripping open its belly and clawing at glistening guts. One of the creatures grabbed the buck's hind leg and twisted it off as easily as if it had been a quail's wing.

On its boulder, the leader swung round, barking furiously. It wasn't barking at Hylas and Pirra.

Hylas' belly turned over.

Havoc was sneaking towards the carcass, intent on scaring away the creatures and seizing their prey, as she might scare away foxes or pine martens.

But these were no foxes.

'Havoc come *back!*' shouted Hylas.

The young lioness knew her name well enough, but she ignored it. She hadn't been fed much on the ship, and a few chunks of snake weren't enough to blunt her hunger. The smell of fresh meat was agonizing.

'Havoc come *back!*' yelled Hylas and Pirra together.

Havoc broke cover and charged, snarling and lashing out with her forepaws. But instead of scattering, the creatures raced *towards* her, barking furiously and gnashing their fangs. And now more of them were emerging from caves higher up, streaming down to join the attack, and the leader was hurtling over the sand at a dreadful shambling run.

Hylas and Pirra ran after him, Hylas yelling and firing pebbles with his slingshot, Pirra flinging whatever rocks she could find.

Havoc realized her mistake, turned tail and fled. Hylas and Pirra did the same.

As he ran, Hylas glanced over his shoulder. The creatures weren't coming after them. They were leaping up and down at the foot of the outcrop, beating the ground with their fists.

Their leader sat on his haunches, glaring at the

intruders who had dared approach his stronghold: *Stay away! Don't come back!*

'*Baboons*,' panted Pirra some time later. 'I knew User-ref had mentioned them, I just couldn't remember the name.'

'Is there a baboon god too?' gasped Hylas.

'I think so. They're incredibly clever and not afraid of anything.'

'I could see that for myself!'

The Sun would be down soon, but the heat was still fierce. They had backtracked all the way down the shore, past where the Phoenicians had left them and where they'd killed the snake, and were now warily approaching another clump of boulders that looked as if it might provide shelter. If it wasn't full of baboons.

With his slingshot, Hylas pelted the outcrop with pebbles.

No angry barks, no vicious dog-men swarming out to attack.

Telling Pirra to wait, he climbed towards what appeared to be the mouth of a cave, flinging rocks as he went, to flush out anything hiding inside. A couple of bats flickered out of the darkness, but nothing else.

'It's clear,' he called down. Dropping his gear, he

crawled inside. It was stifling, but any shade was a relief after the Sun.

Pirra crawled in too, and slumped on to her side. Her face was filmed with dust and sweat. When she peeled off her sandals, the thongs left her feet marked with red stripes.

The Sea wasn't far away, but they were too exhausted to stagger down and wash. What strength Hylas had left, he would need for setting snares.

He went outside again. From this vantage-point, he saw a low rocky ridge not far off, and beyond it, the endless red desert, stretching to the end of the world.

The wind carried weird yelping calls. He wondered if they were jackals. He guessed that whatever creatures lived in the desert would hide from the Sun and come out at night. That was why Havoc, feeling the onset of dusk, had plodded off to hunt. Hylas only hoped she had the sense to stalk lizards or hares – if there were any – and stay away from baboons.

Behind him, Pirra coughed, and clawed at her dust-caked hair. 'How much water's left?'

Hylas hefted the waterskin, then set it down again at the mouth of the cave. 'Enough for a day. Maybe two.'

She took that in silence, running her tongue over her chapped lips.

'We'll rest for a bit,' he said, 'but we can't sleep here all night.'

'Why not?'

'The Sun, Pirra. We made a mistake, walking in daylight. From now on, we'll have to move by night, or we'll burn up.'

'And go where?' she mumbled. 'West again, and hope we can sneak past those baboons? Or keep going east, and pray that the river's this way?'

Hylas didn't answer. Neither sounded like much of a plan.

Taking what was left of the snake from his belt, he chucked it to her. 'I'll go and gather some of that scrub and wake up a fire.'

She glanced at the mangled carcass. 'I'm not hungry.'

'We need to eat. It'll taste better cooked.'

The Sun was a bloody ball of fire sinking towards the horizon, but the heat was still crushing. As Hylas picked his way down the rocks, the ridge before him danced in the heat, and behind him, his shadow, stretching over the stones, was weirdly misshapen.

'What happens if we don't find anything,' called Pirra. 'Just more and more desert?'

'I don't know,' he replied.

Out of the corner of his eye, he saw his shadow take on a life of its own.

It took Hylas a moment to realize that it wasn't his shadow, it was a boy, as dark as a shadow.

But by then the boy had snatched the waterskin and fled.

3

The thief sped towards the ridge with the waterskin over his shoulder. If he got amongst those boulders, he'd be gone for good.

Hylas raced after him, whirling his slingshot over his head. The thief fell with a yelp, clutching his shin. Hylas jumped him and tried to pin him by the arms, but he was strong, twisting round and aiming a knee at Hylas' groin. Hylas dodged, jabbed an elbow at his throat. With a choking cough, the thief squirmed out from under. Hylas grabbed his hair, but it was short as a shorn ram's, he couldn't get a grip. The thief scrambled to his feet and whipped a flint knife from a sheath strapped to his upper arm. Slashing the air before him, he backed towards the boulders – still with the waterskin over his shoulder.

'Drop the waterskin!' panted Hylas, drawing his own knife and showing the thief its lethal bronze blade. 'I don't want to kill you but I will!'

The thief snarled something in a tongue Hylas didn't know and edged closer to the boulders.

Pirra ran round to cut off his escape. The thief flung out a hand and sent her flying, then fled for the rocks with Hylas in pursuit.

Suddenly Hylas caught movement on the ridge – and there was Havoc, gazing down at the thief. The thief howled in terror and sped sideways. In two effortless bounds, Havoc was on him.

'Throw away your knife!' yelled Hylas.

'I'll try it in Egyptian,' shouted Pirra, then yelled something Hylas couldn't understand.

Havoc lay on top of her quarry, playfully batting his head between her forepaws while he flailed like a beetle on its back. Luckily for him, she wasn't in earnest and had sheathed her claws.

'If you don't throw away your knife,' snarled Hylas, 'I'll tell my lion to bare her claws!'

With a hiss, the thief tossed his knife aside. Hylas kicked it out of reach, then grabbed the waterskin and chucked it to Pirra. 'Seems he does understand Akean, after all.'

'What's your name?' Pirra demanded in Akean.

The boy merely glared at her.

She said something in what Hylas guessed was Egyptian. Still no response. She flung up her arms. 'Why doesn't he answer?'

'Because it's safer to say nothing,' said Hylas. 'It's what I'd do in his place.'

They'd dragged him back to the cave, Pirra having run and fetched the rope, with which Hylas had tied his arms. Night had fallen with startling suddenness, and they'd woken a small scrubwood fire. The thief huddled at the back of the cave, eyeing Havoc, who sat at the entrance, snuffing his scent. He seemed wary, but no longer terrified – which meant he was either brave, or a fool. Something about his bearing told Hylas that he wasn't a fool.

He seemed to be about Hylas' own age, and his skin wasn't black, as Hylas had thought, but the rich dark brown of polished walnut wood. Hylas had never seen anyone so dark. His wiry black hair clung close to his skull, and lines of straight ridged scars on his high cheekbones seemed to have been done on purpose. His horny feet were bare, and he wore nothing but a rag tied round his hips. His jagged flint knife was familiar enough. Hylas had carried a similar one for most of his life; but thrust in his belt was a bent piece of wood like two sides of a triangle. Hylas had never seen such a weapon.

With a jerk of her head, Pirra drew him aside. 'D'you think there are others like him out here?' she said.

'Let's hope not,' he muttered, 'or we're in even more trouble than we thought. But what *is* he? He's not Egyptian, I know that much. Have you ever seen skin that dark?'

She nodded. 'Sometimes they come to Keftiu to trade. They're desert people, from a country near Egypt. Incredibly tough, amazing archers. But they're supposed to be *brave*,' she added loudly, so that the boy could hear. 'Only a coward would steal our waterskin.'

That had its effect, and the boy glowered at her.

Putting her head close to Hylas', she dropped her voice to a whisper. 'What do we *do* with him? We can't leave him tied up, but if we let him go . . .'

Hylas went and stood over the boy. 'Are you alone?' he said brusquely.

The boy turned his head away. The muscles of his arms bulged as he clenched his fists.

Hylas saw that his back was criss-crossed with scars: not the orderly ridges on his cheeks, but the scars you got from beatings. Hylas knew about those – he had some of his own.

They gave him an idea. Hunkering down on his heels, he met the boy's eyes. 'You were a slave,' he said quietly.

Nothing moved in the surly brown face.

'I was a slave once,' said Hylas. Holding out his forearm, he showed the boy his zigzag tattoo. 'That's the mark of my enemies. A powerful clan in a land called Akea, far to the north. People call them the Crows.' The boy's eyelids flickered. Did he know the name? The mark?

'Crows,' repeated Hylas. 'Two summers ago I was a goatherd on Mount Lykas. That's a mountain in Akea. The Crows attacked my camp and killed my dog. My sister went missing. I was twelve, she was nine. My best friend Telamon turned out to be a Crow.' He swallowed. He hadn't intended to say so much. 'The Crows caught me and made me a slave,' he went on. 'They made me work in their mines. But I ran away.' He let that sink in. 'I think you ran away too.'

The boy's face remained stubbornly blank, but Hylas knew he was listening. 'What's your name?' he said.

A long pause. 'Kem,' growled the boy. 'That the name they give I.' His voice was rough with contempt. 'It mean – black. And I *not* a coward!'

'What's your real name?' said Pirra.

Kem shot her an incredulous look. *Why would I tell you?*

'So we'll call you Kem,' said Hylas. 'Where are you heading?'

Another pause. 'My country. You call it Wawat. Egyptians call it Land of Black Stranger.'

'What do *you* call it?' said Hylas.

Kem spat something incomprehensible.

'How long have you been a runaway?' said Hylas.

Kem shrugged. 'Five, six day.'

'Your country,' said Pirra. 'Where is it?'

'South of Egypt,' said Kem. 'Long, long way upriver.'

Hylas and Pirra exchanged glances. 'Do you mean the Great River?' said Pirra. 'The one Egyptians call Iteru-aa?'

Kem started at her as if she was an idiot. 'Of course! What other river there is in the world?'

Pirra bristled, but Hylas got in first. 'Then we're going the same way. We need to find the River too.'

'*So?*' snarled Kem.

'We're trying to find our friend,' said Hylas. 'He's an Egyptian called Userref. He has something we need.'

'But we don't know where he is,' put in Pirra. 'All we know is he's from somewhere called Pa-Sobek and he has a brother called Nebetku, who's a scribe.'

Kem gave a disbelieving snort. 'That all you know, yet you say you're *friends*?'

Pirra glared at him. 'He was sold as a slave when he was a boy, and he missed his family terribly, it upset him to talk of them – not that that's anything to do with you!'

'All right, Pirra,' said Hylas. Then to Kem: 'Can you get us to Pa-Sobek?'

'Why should I?' snapped Kem.

'Because if you don't,' said Hylas, 'we'll leave you here tied up and you'll die of thirst.'

Kem's dark eyes drilled into his, trying to see if he was bluffing. 'But I know the desert and you don't. You leave me here, you dead too.'

Hylas nodded slowly. 'True. But you see, Kem, you really do need us just as much as we need you.'

Another snort. 'Why so?'

For answer, Hylas called to Havoc, and the young lioness padded over and rubbed against him. She gave a cavernous yawn, baring enormous fangs. Hylas placed his hand on her massive golden head and turned to Kem, who couldn't quite conceal his awe. 'Because,' Hylas said pleasantly, 'if you don't help us reach Pa-Sobek, Havoc here is going to get very, *very* hungry.'

They locked gazes. Again Kem tried to guess if

Hylas was bluffing. Then he threw back his head and barked a laugh. 'So! We help each other. Yes?'

'How come you speak Akean?' said Hylas, wiping snake grease off his chin.

Kem held up three fingers. 'Three years hacking salt in the mines. My friend, he from your country. He drown dead in the lake when we escape.' His voice was level. If he was sad, he gave no sign of it.

'I'm sorry,' said Hylas.

Pirra didn't say anything. She didn't like Kem. He treated her as if she was some idiot girl to be ignored. 'I never heard of anyone mining salt,' she said suspiciously.

'Not salt like the Sea,' retorted Kem. 'This sacred salt, Egyptians call it *hesmen*. They use it for everything – wash, heal, cover their dead so they live for ever.' He prised a shred of meat from between his strong white teeth. 'But for my friend, no *hesmen*. They chuck out his body for jackals to eat.'

'That's bad,' said Hylas.

Kem hawked and spat. 'The only people who matter to Egyptians are Egyptians. People from foreign, like us from Wawat, they think we not human.'

This was too much for Pirra. 'Userref is Egyptian,' she said hotly, 'and he's not like that!'

'Oh no?' sneered Kem.

'No!'

'For true? Who this Userref? He give you that scar?'

'Shut up about my scar!' she shouted.

'Stop it, both of you,' said Hylas.

Sensing that Pirra was upset, Echo flew in and settled on her shoulder. Havoc ambled over and leant against her, giving Kem a hard stare. Clearly, she also disliked this stranger in their midst.

Kem's eyes flicked from Havoc to Hylas, to Pirra. He barked his mirthless laugh. 'First, I thought you were gods. You with the lion, she with the hawk.'

'Falcon,' Pirra said coldly. 'And that didn't stop you stealing our waterskin.'

'No, but it stopped me killing you for it.'

She opened her mouth to reply, but Hylas spoke first. 'How long will it take to reach the Great River, Kem?'

The dark boy shrugged. 'Three–four days, if you do what I say.' His mouth twisted in a grin. 'Lotta danger in the desert. Leopard, scorpion. You must be *brave*,' he added with a glance at Pirra.

'What's a scorpion?' she said between her teeth.

For answer, Kem snatched a stick from the fire, rooted around at the back of the cave, bashed something with a rock, then returned with it dangling from the stick. 'This a scorpion.' He waved it in her face.

She forced herself not to flinch. It was like a tiny black crayfish with a vicious-looking sting curled over its back. 'Very impressive,' she said drily. 'Now tell us how to reach Pa-Sobek.'

'Oh, it *easy*,' Kem said sarcastically, chucking the scorpion in the fire. 'First we cross the desert, then we get past the border guards. They watch for barbarians, runaway slaves. They get paid for each kill they can prove.'

'Go on,' said Hylas.

Kem looked at them angrily. 'Here. I make you to know what is Egypt!' With his finger, he drew an upside-down triangle in the sand, tapering to a long vertical line; it made Pirra think of a flower on a very long stalk. Kem pointed at the flat top of the triangle. 'This the Sea. This,' he outlined the triangle, 'the mouth of the River. They call it Ta-Mehi, the Great Green. Huge papyrus marsh, lotta dangery animals: cobra, river horse, crocodile.' His eyes met Pirra's. 'You know what is crocodile?'

'Of course,' she snapped.

He gave a disbelieving snort. 'After Great Green, the River Valley.' He ran his finger all the way down the stalk. 'Very long, very dangery. River look sleepy, but it got rocks, currents, sandbanks. More river horse, more crocodile – and everywhere people: warrior, headmen, overseer. Egyptians got plenty food, but they always being counted and watched: how many crop you got? Where you going? Lotta boats on the River, but if a stranger ship try to go upstream, maybe one with big black sail, oh, they know it quick time!' Lastly, he stabbed a point right at the bottom of the stalk. 'There. Pa-Sobek.'

Pirra swallowed. 'And your country – Wawat – that's south of Pa-Sobek?'

Kem nodded.

Hylas was running his thumb over his bottom lip. 'Where are we now?'

Kem jabbed at a point right up by the Sea and left of the Great Green. 'Here.'

Silence. Pirra heard the crackle of the fire – and outside, the vast silence of the desert.

Hylas sat cross-legged with his hands on his knees. 'Why did you mention strangers' ships?' he asked quietly.

Pirra threw him a puzzled glance.

Kem shrugged. 'You go to Pa-Sobek, you need to steal a boat –'

'But you said strangers' ships with big black sails,' said Hylas. 'You were thinking of one in particular, weren't you?'

Kem met that with one of his stubborn silences.

'Kem,' said Hylas. 'There's something you're not telling us.' He tapped the Crow tattoo on his forearm. 'You've seen this before. Haven't you?'

Kem stirred. Then he seemed to come to a decision. 'Word travel, even among slaves. While ago, I hear tell of a stranger ship from Akea, the land of my friend. Black sails. Warriors. Bronze weapon, black cloak, mark like yours on they shield.'

Pirra couldn't breathe. She smelt again the stink of warrior sweat and the bitter tang of the ash the Crows smeared on their skin.

In the leaping light, Hylas' face was haunted. He was fingering the scar on his upper arm, where he'd dug out a Crow arrowhead two summers before. 'Did you learn what they were after?' he said hoarsely.

Again Kem shrugged. 'People say they bring bronze for the Perao – Perao, he the headman of all Egypt. He need bronze to fight his enemies. So the ship come and Perao he take the bronze, and he let them go upriver –'

'When?' cut in Pirra. 'How long ago did the ship get here?'

'Long time,' said Kem.

'How long?' cried Hylas and Pirra together.

'Nearly two moons.'

4

Telamon whipped the horses and sent his chariot thundering after his quarry. The antelopes were straining every sinew as they raced across the desert – but he was gaining on them, and a doe was falling behind.

Passing reins and whip to Ilarkos, Telamon nocked an arrow to his bow. It struck the oryx in the neck and she fell, crashing head over hooves.

Ilarkos hauled the horses to a halt in clouds of red dust, and Telamon leapt down and finished her off with his knife.

'Good shot, my lord,' panted Ilarkos.

Telamon wanted to shout his triumph to the sky – but that would be boyish, so he just gave a curt nod.

The hunting party ran up, carrying his other kills: an ostrich, a leopard, and her two cubs.

Not bad for a morning's hunt, thought Telamon. He nudged the oryx with his foot. 'I only want the horn,' he told Ilarkos. 'See to it. I'm heading back.'

As the Sun rose, he thundered across the desert: through the gap in the great rocky ridge that loomed over the West Bank, past the fields and huddled villages of peasants and tomb-builders, and down to the River's edge, where the Hati-aa's barge was waiting.

Leaving the chariot and the exhausted horses for slaves to lead to the stables, he strode up the landing-plank and barked at the oarsmen to take him across to Pa-Sobek.

His spirits were high as he settled himself under the canopy, and he ran his hand along his jaw to feel his new beard, which was finally starting to grow. Yanking off his helmet, he admired its rows of ivory plaques sliced from the tusks of boars.

'My *helmet*,' he said proudly. He'd killed all twelve boars himself, and with the last, he'd become a man and a warrior.

He glanced at Pirra's sealstone on his wrist, with its tiny amethyst falcon. 'You sneered at me,' he told her under his breath. 'You called me a "Crow". But I won't be insulted, Pirra. I'm not a "Crow", I'm a warrior of the House of Koronos. The Perao of all Egypt grants me safe-conduct, and the ruler of Pa-Sobek gives me a feast every night. What do you think of that?'

The East Bank was approaching, and before him lay Pa-Sobek, surrounded by green orchards and rich fields. He saw its tall white houses and bustling marketplace, shaded by the strange spiky trees they called date-palms; its stone jetty and tree-lined avenue guarded by giant basalt falcons – and beyond, its vast, secretive walled Temple.

Further along the bank lay the Hati-aa's palace. It was far larger and more magnificent than Mycenae, where Telamon's grandfather ruled – and yet it wasn't even the main palace, that was upstream, on the border with Wawat. This one, in which Telamon and Alekto were increasingly impatient guests, was only where the Hati-aa stayed when he wished to be near the Temple.

But Telamon refused to be intimidated. He despised all Egyptians. They might be unimaginably rich, but they weren't proper warriors. The Hati-aa had a garrison of men, but they didn't wear helmets or armour, and until a few years ago, their weapons had been soft copper instead of bronze.

And the Hati-aa seemed more interested in plants.

He kept slaves whose sole task was to tend trees and flowers and a fishpond in what he called a 'garden'. He even had a smaller 'garden' in the courtyard *inside* the palace. *Why?* What *for*?

As for the Hati-aa himself, Telamon hadn't seen him since he'd fallen ill and had left the care of his guests to his young wife, Meritamen. What kind of man leaves a girl of fourteen in charge?

Swallows were swooping over the courtyard as Telamon strode into the palace. Columns carved like papyrus flowers, cool passages tiled in green and yellow, a floor of polished gypsum, strewn with sweet clover to keep away flies.

The 'garden' before him was bright with pomegranate trees and blue cornflowers. White waterlilies floated in a green marble pool. The Hati-aa's wife and her little sister were playing with their pets. As Telamon entered, they stopped and stared.

The little sister was six. Her head was shaven but for a braid at the temple, and she wore nothing except a blue bead belt. Telamon had never seen her without her cat.

The Hati-aa's wife, Meritamen, was pretty in a way that reminded Telamon of the gazelle at her heels. She had large dark eyes rimmed with black, a fringe across her brow, and many tiny braids down her back.

Her narrow dress of finely pleated white linen set off her smooth brown shoulders and hennaed feet.

To show her he was at ease, Telamon set his helmet on the ground and washed his head and hands in the pool.

The little sister scooped her cat into her arms and backed away. Meritamen placed a protective hand on her sister's head. 'Did you have a good hunt, Lord Tel-amon?' she said quietly. She was the only member of the household who spoke Akean, having learnt it from her nurse. But she rarely looked Telamon in the face, which annoyed him. He was handsome, why couldn't she see that?

'A leopard and two cubs,' he replied, wringing out his long warrior braids.

Suddenly, the child gave a muffled giggle. Merita-men glanced sideways – and gasped.

Telamon froze. The gazelle had just spattered a neat pile of pellets in his upturned helmet.

His blood roared in his ears. 'The filthy . . .' He lashed out with his foot, but the creature skittered off down a passage.

The little sister was desperately smothering her giggles in her cat's fur. On the balcony above them, a slave snorted and clamped his hands to his mouth.

Meritamen was aghast. 'I am – sorry, Lord Tel-amon.'

She snapped a command at a slave girl, who rushed forwards and shook out his helmet.

Telamon snatched it and stalked off, the laughter of slaves and women ringing in his ears.

It seemed to take ages to mount the stairs to the men's quarters. In his chamber, he tore off his sweat-soiled tunic and shouted for water and wine. He'd never hated Egypt as intensely as he did now. Everyone looking down at him and laughing.

Even that slave, Userref, had laughed. Bloodied and beaten, he'd laughed his defiance in Telamon's face. And in the end he'd found a way to escape.

And now the days were slipping by like the sands of this cursed desert, and Telamon was no closer to finding the dagger.

'What did you slaughter this time?' murmured Alekto as they sat together at the feast. 'Did you finally kill a lion?'

Telamon bristled. She knew he hadn't, she just wanted to make him say it. 'I killed a leopard,' he told her. 'Like your beloved plaything.'

She laughed. The other day, her leopard had scratched her hand, and she'd had its throat cut.

'Have you made any progress?' snapped Telamon.

Alekto turned her head to accept a fig from Kerasher

with a smile that made the Egyptian break out in a sweat. 'I thought I had,' she told Telamon. 'My slave found a peasant who seemed promising, but his heart gave out.' At the memory, she drew her lips back from her teeth in a way that was half smile and half grimace. She only smiled like that when she thought of pain – or, better still, when she observed it: beatings, wounds probed and stitched, the more agonizing the better. As long as there was pain.

Tonight she looked particularly beautiful, in a robe of scarlet silk and a sash of gilded calfskin, with gold snakes entwined in her dark hair. Telamon hated and feared her, but he understood now that his grandfather had been right to send her with him instead of Pharax. 'Force won't help you in Egypt,' Koronos had said. 'Egyptians admire beauty. Alekto will be more use to you than Pharax.'

Telamon had been daunted. 'But how will we persuade them to find the dagger?' And how would he survive in Egypt, that mysterious, unimaginably rich land at the end of the world, with only one ship and forty men?

'The Perao wields enormous power,' Koronos had said, 'but not even he is secure. A few years ago, he rid his land of foreigners from the east – with my help. His army needed bronze, and I sold it to him. You will take him more bronze, and in return he will help you find the dagger.'

It had worked. With a shipful of bronze, Telamon had bought his way through the marshlands to the Perao's astonishing palace of Waset, where the god-king Himself had granted them safe-conduct and Kerasher's assistance. And Kerasher's spies had tracked the slave Userref here to Pa-Sobek, the southern-most province of Egypt. But that had been over a moon ago.

A naked slave girl offered Telamon a dish of doum-palm nuts. He waved her away, then barked at her to bring drink.

Spiced pomegranate wine in a turquoise cup painted with black lotus flowers. Telamon forced it down. He was sick of feasts. The flutes, the incense, the ostrich-feather fans and the dancing girls' bright naked limbs. Even the roast oxen drenched in cinnamon and sesame, and the rich white bread sweetened with dates.

He thought of the Perao's safe-conduct: woven reeds they called a 'scroll', painted with tiny meaning-less pictures that made him feel stupid. He didn't want scrolls, he wanted the dagger of Koronos: to feel its power stiffening his sinews and kindling a fire in his blood . . .

'I hear your helmet met with an accident,' said Alekto.

Telamon threw her a cold look. 'What have you done all day, apart from torturing peasants?'

With her fingernail, she slit the dusky skin of the fig and sniffed its purple flesh. 'Meritamen is young and inexperienced. But I think she knows something.'

'Why didn't you find out sooner?'

'Be patient, nephew –'

'I'm sick of being patient!' Telamon slammed down his cup with a crash that stopped the music and turned heads around the hall. 'This has gone on long enough! From now on, we do it my way!'

'I won't wait any longer,' said Telamon when the hall had been cleared of all except Alekto, Kerasher and Meritamen, who sat tensely in the Hati-aa's ebony chair. 'I'm convinced that our dagger is in the Temple,' Telamon went on. 'No more delay. You must have it searched.'

Meritamen glanced at Kerasher, who gave her a weary smile, as if Telamon had said something particularly stupid. 'Noble Lord Telamon,' he began. 'Not even I or the Lady Meritamen may do that. We may not even *enter* the Temple! Only priests – servants of the gods – are allowed within. And they swear they do not have your amulet.'

'Dagger,' corrected Telamon.

The Egyptian acknowledged his error with a bow that was almost a shrug.

Alekto spoke to Meritamen. 'Please tell me why, if the dagger isn't in the Temple, there's so much coming and going around it?'

Telamon resented her butting in. And Meritamen's answer was infuriatingly off the point. 'Every year,' she said carefully, 'the gods cause the Great River to rise. This takes many days, but at last the River covers the land. We call this Akhet: the Time of the Flood.'

Telamon stirred impatiently.

'When the waters finally recede,' Meritamen went on, 'they leave our fields covered in rich black mud. Thus Egypt is reborn, as it has been every year since the beginning –'

'What's this got to do with the dagger?' broke in Telamon.

'The start of the Flood,' said Kerasher, 'is the start of the New Year: the most important time. We hold a great *heb*, a festival. The *heb* of the First Drop is only a few days away.'

'Which is why,' Meritamen said patiently, 'there is so much coming and going in the Temple.'

'But surely,' said Alekto, 'as ruler of Pa-Sobek in your husband's place, you can order the priests –'

'Ah no!' chuckled Kerasher, waving with his ebony fly-whisk. 'The priests don't serve the Lady Meritamen – they serve the gods!'

Telamon was struggling to keep his temper. 'I don't think either of you understands. I am the grandson of Koronos, High Chieftain of Mycenae. The Lady Alekto is the High Chieftain's daughter.'

Meritamen looked at him in puzzlement. 'But – this we know . . .'

'Allow me to go on,' Telamon said between his teeth.

She licked her lips. Kerasher's smile faltered.

'The Perao has decreed that we must regain our dagger,' continued Telamon. 'With the help of Lord Kerasher, we traced it here to Pa-Sobek. But you have failed to find it.'

Good. Neither Egyptian was smiling now.

'If, by the time your River begins to rise,' said Telamon, 'I do not hold the dagger in my fist, the Perao will know that His decree has been ignored.' He paused. 'That will be your fault, Lady Meritamen. It won't matter who you are. The Perao needs bronze more than he needs you, or the Hati-aa. One word from my grandfather, and you will be punished.

Against the wrath of the Perao, you and your family will be as a field of flax in a sandstorm. You will be wiped out.'

Kerasher was regarding Telamon with new respect. Tiny beads of sweat had broken out on Meritamen's upper lip, and she was staring at Telamon in horror.

He rose to leave. 'Think about that,' he told her.

As Telamon was about to mount the stairs to his chamber, Meritamen motioned him aside.

Around them slaves were clearing away the remains of the feast. She led Telamon to an empty side-chamber. Its walls were painted with blue and yellow waterbirds, and beside a cedarwood chair stood a lampstand of white alabaster, burning sweet-scented oil.

'Well?' said Telamon. He was surprised that she wished to talk to him without Kerasher. She'd never done that before.

Meritamen twisted her small hennaed hands. 'I cannot let this bring down my family,' she said quietly.

'Then find the dagger. Alekto thinks you know something.'

She blinked. 'If I knew where it was, I would give it to you. But I don't.'

'Then find out.'

When she didn't answer, he said, 'Why are you speaking to me without Kerasher?'

She hesitated. 'Kerasher answers only to the Perao Himself. His spies are not from here – from Pa-Sobek.'

Telamon caught his breath. 'Why do I get the feeling that you know something?'

She frowned. 'This dagger – *why* is it so important?'

'As long as we have it, my clan can't be beaten.' He didn't mention the prophecy which said that if an Outsider wielded the dagger, the House of Koronos would fall. Hylas was that Outsider: the very boy who'd once been his best friend. But he, Telamon, was destined to kill Hylas and save his clan.

'We would give you this dagger if we could,' said Meritamen. 'But we don't have it!'

'I don't believe you. The slave Userref – he was born in Pa-Sobek. There must be friends of his, family . . .'

'Why cannot you return to your own land, and if we find it, we will send it to you?'

'Because others seek it too: people who want to destroy it and bring down my clan.'

'What people?'

'A boy,' he said between his teeth. 'Yellow hair, part of one earlobe cut off. A Keftian girl with a scar like a crescent moon on her cheek. They are my enemies.

I have sworn to kill them.' He pictured Hylas and Pirra as he'd last seen them: Pirra magnificent in the purple robes of her dead mother, with live snakes coiled about her arms and a falcon flying to her aid. Hylas bloodied and embattled, with a young lioness leaping to his defence.

'I don't believe they can get as far as Egypt,' he said, as much to reassure himself as to tell Meritamen. 'But if your spies should ever hear of them, you must tell me at once. Do you understand?'

Meritamen nodded slowly. Raising her head, she looked at him. 'I will not let this ruin my family,' she said with surprising determination. 'Kerasher does not care about the people of Pa-Sobek. I do. I will find your dagger. Kerasher does not need to know how.'

'What about –'

'You do not need to know either, my Lord Tel-amon. I will bring you your dagger. But you must allow me to protect my people, and do it my way.'

5

Moonlight glinted in Hylas' fair hair as he
fell into step beside Pirra. 'Kem says we're
not far from the Great Green.'

She snorted. 'And you believe him?'

'Well if it wasn't for him, we'd dead by now.'

Pirra hated to admit it, but he was right. For three
nights and three dawns, Kem had led them tirelessly
through the desert. He'd made them smear charcoal
under their eyes to cut down the glare, and given them
each a pebble to put in their mouths against thirst.
Somehow, he'd scratched together enough food
to keep them alive: bitter roots, nubbly thorn bush
leaves, and once, to Pirra's disgust, a porcupine.
Tonight he was tracking something bigger. He hadn't
told them what.

She still didn't trust him. 'For all we know, he's leading us straight into one of those border patrols he keeps going on about.'

'Why would he do that?' snapped Hylas. 'They'd only catch him too.'

She didn't reply. She was sick of being hungry and thirsty, and her sandals were giving her blisters, but she dared not go barefoot because of scorpions. She was also desperately worried about Userref. The Crows had been in Egypt for so long. What if they'd found him? In her mind, she saw him beaten and tortured. She couldn't bear it.

Hylas touched her shoulder. 'Look! Kem's found tracks.'

Up ahead, Kem was squatting to examine the sand, his dark skin almost invisible in the gloom.

'As long as it's not another porcupine,' muttered Pirra.

Furiously, Kem motioned her to be quiet, then pointed with his throwstick and jerked his head at Hylas to follow – ignoring Pirra, whom he regarded as useless in a hunt.

Havoc had also sensed prey. Silver in the moonlight, the young lioness was creeping out to the left, to help in the ambush. She moved noiselessly, her head sunk low between her shoulder blades. Suddenly, she froze with one forepaw lifted.

Pirra caught movement in the distance. As quietly as she could, she joined Hylas.

He stood aghast. 'What *are* they?' he whispered. 'They look like *giant birds*!'

They were taller than men, and they planted their huge spiked feet with exaggerated care, bending long pale necks to peck the sand.

'I think they're ostriches,' hissed Pirra. She thought of the giant eggs in the House of the Goddess, and her belly rumbled. 'I hope they're good to eat.'

Hylas was gone, moving silently round to the right. With Havoc to the left and Kem in the middle, the ambush was complete. Pirra drew her knife and wondered which way to go.

Suddenly, one of the ostriches jerked up its head. Now the whole flock was off, racing over the sand at incredible speed. They were heading for Hylas. He and Kem broke cover and ran towards them, Hylas firing his slingshot, Kem casting his throwstick. The great birds were too fast. They veered round, heading for Havoc. She lay low, ready to pounce. They hadn't seen her, and the lead ostrich was almost within reach. One swipe and she'd bring it down . . .

But Havoc had never seen giant birds before, and she lost her nerve and fled.

Again the flock turned, and this time, Pirra ran

forwards to head them off. She heard the thud of Kem's throwstick and his angry cry as it fell short. More pebbles from Hylas' slingshot, also falling short. The flock was hurtling towards her. Clutching her knife, she stood her ground.

Before she could lash out, the lead bird thundered past, then the others. The last was coming straight at her.

'Get outta the way!' yelled Kem.

Still Pirra stood her ground. She saw the bird's powerful legs striking the ground like hammers. She saw its big spiky feet. It was only a bird, surely it wouldn't run her down?

Yes it would. She threw herself sideways, and the ostrich sped past her in a hail of grit.

'What were you *doing*?' panted Kem. 'One kick and it cuts you open like a watermelon!'

'You could've told me that before!' snarled Pirra.

Throwing up his arms, Kem stomped off.

'Thanks for standing up for me,' Pirra told Hylas as he helped her to her feet.

He ignored that. 'Are you hurt?' he panted.

'No,' she lied. She was bruised and had scraped one knee. She was also embarrassed. She hated confirming Kem's view that girls were no use.

Havoc was embarrassed too. Bounding over to Hylas, she rubbed against him, making groany *yowmp-yowmp* noises and seeking reassurance. He sighed. 'This isn't right. She should be getting *braver* as she grows up, but she's getting worse.'

'Well, she'll just have to learn,' Pirra said crossly.

'But she's nearly two, Pirra. By now she should be bringing down big prey on her own. She can't survive on lizards.' Hunkering down, he scratched behind Havoc's ears. 'You're not a cub any more, Havoc, you're nearly full-grown. Don't you know that?'

Pirra felt a flash of sympathy for the young lioness. 'She's been through so much. Maybe she's lost her nerve.'

Hylas nodded sadly. In Havoc's short life, she'd lost her father and mother, been through fire, earthshake, the Great Wave, and a terrible winter all on her own. 'And now this desert,' he said. 'Baboons, cobras, those hyaenas last night . . .'

'She'll learn.'

'She'll have to, and fast.' He looked at Pirra. 'If she doesn't find her courage soon, she'll never be able to hunt by herself. She'll never grow up. She'll never be a proper lion.'

Angry and ashamed, the lion cub slunk off into the Dark.

She *hated* this place. The burning sand bit her pads,

and the flies never left her alone. There was nothing to drink and almost no trees – her claws were aching for a good scratch – and that black boy who'd attached himself to the pride kept distracting *her* boy, so that, sometimes, he forgot to give her a muzzle-rub.

Worse even than that, she was *scared*. Snakes that spat. Furry not-men that barked and gnashed their teeth. And now these monster birds . . . A while ago, she'd come upon a pack of dogs feasting on a deer, and had tried to chase them away – but *they* had chased *her*. They were the weirdest dogs she'd ever seen, with sloping backs covered in spots, and horrible sneaky laughs. What kind of a dog *laughs*?

The wind carried a new scent to her nose: hare. Well at least that was something she knew.

The scent-trail ended, weirdly, in a thorn tree. The lion cub smelt that the hare was right up in its branches. This was extremely odd. She didn't know that hares could climb trees.

She leapt at the trunk – but a savage growl warned her back.

From high in the tree, a lion glared down at her. No, not a lion. It was smaller, with a different smell, *and its pelt was covered in black spots.*

The spotted almost-lion bared its fangs and hissed at her. *This is my kill, get away!*

Hungry and humiliated, the lion cub slunk off to find her humans.

Lions shouldn't be frightened of dogs, or of smaller lions (even if they do have spots), and they definitely shouldn't be scared of birds.

This was a horrible place. The lion cub didn't belong.

To begin with, the falcon had liked this place. She'd liked the red and purple sand rushing beneath her, and she'd had fun playing all over the vast, empty Sky.

But she'd soon realized that she didn't belong. It was far too hot, and no matter how thoroughly she preened, she couldn't get the dust out of her feathers. She'd tried bathing in the Sea, but that only made her sticky, and a sand-bath was worse, as it was full of ants, and the falcon had been terrified of ants since she was a fledgling and had fallen out of the Nest.

It didn't help that her humans had taken to moving about in the Dark, when they should've been roosting. This meant that instead of having a nice quiet roost herself, the falcon had to keep flying off to find them – although as they were earthbound and slow, that never took long.

But the worst thing about this place was that there were no birds to eat, so she had to demean herself by hunting tough little lizards and dusty mice. Once, she'd spotted a bat, but as she was chasing it towards a crag, she'd been attacked by a grown-up falcon. *That's my bat!* it had screeched. *These are my rocks! Stay away!*

Tilting one wingfeather, the falcon rolled on to the Wind and let it carry her closer to the Moon.

She spotted movement below. When she saw what it was, she was so horrified she nearly fell off the Wind.

There *were* birds down there, but something was dreadfully wrong. These birds were bigger than deer – and they were running over the ground, flapping tiny, useless wings. *These birds couldn't fly.*

It was the worst thing the falcon had ever seen, it made her feel sick and fluttery inside. Shrieking, she wheeled across the Sky to find the girl. The girl would understand. She might be earthbound and human, but her spirit was as fierce as any falcon's, and at times, she and the falcon felt the same things.

It wasn't long before the falcon found her. As she settled on the girl's wrist and heard that slow, gentle human voice, the fluttering inside her ceased.

It helped, too, that in her other hand, the girl was holding a shard of white shell full of the falcon's absolute favourite food: delicious yellow egg. The falcon sipped hungrily – while keeping a wary eye out for the lion cub, who'd got much better about not sneaking up on her, but occasionally forgot. However, it turned out that the lion cub also loved eggs, and was busy crunching up several of her own.

By the time everyone had eaten, the Sun was waking up and the falcon felt much better. After a swift preen and an affectionate tug at the girl's hair, she flew off again to take a look around.

As she let a hot updraught carry her higher, she saw that in the distance, the dry red lands came to an end in a blaze of brilliant green.

The roots of her feathers tightened with excitement. No more hunting lizards, no more ghastly flightless birds. Amongst the green, the falcon caught the flicker of many wings. Ducks, doves, pigeons . . . Far more than she'd ever seen.

Then, at the edge of the great green, she spotted something else, and slid sideways across the Sky to take a look.

Men. Men with long flying claws that glinted in the Sun.

And her own humans were heading straight for them.

6

'What's bothering Echo?' said Hylas as they started after Kem.

'Maybe there are more ostriches about,' said Pirra. 'They bother me, too. Birds that can't fly, ugh, it feels all wrong!'

'Well I'm not sorry we found those eggs,' said Hylas. It felt marvellous to be full. Behind him, Havoc ambled along with her belly sagging almost to the ground, having devoured four giant eggs all by herself.

'Keep up!' urged Kem in a hoarse whisper. 'And careful in the rocks! Lotta horned vipers in there!'

Pirra rolled her eyes. 'And of course they can't just be *ordinary* vipers,' she said as they followed him over the broken ground. 'Oh no, they've got to have *horns*, because everything here is so much more *dangery* than what we're used to!'

She was furious with Kem, because earlier, he'd asked her again how she'd come by her scar. 'If you must know,' she'd snapped, 'I did it to make myself ugly, so that my mother couldn't marry me off to some chieftain I'd never met. Satisfied?'

But Kem had shaken his head in disbelief. '*Ugly?* Tcha! Not where I come from!'

Pirra had thought he was laughing at her, and when Hylas had tried to explain that he wasn't, she'd turned on *him*. 'Whose side are you on?'

The sky was starting to lighten, but ahead of them Kem went scrambling up the rocks, which led to a stony ridge, dotted with thornscrub.

Behind them, Havoc grunted. She stood with her ears pricked and her tail high, snuffing the air. Then she bounded after Kem.

'What's she smelt?' said Pirra.

'I don't know,' said Hylas. 'But she isn't scared. She's eager.'

Kem swiftly reached the top, and waved at them to hurry.

At last, Hylas crested the ridge. He gasped.

Below him, the desert ended abruptly in a narrow

strip of red sand, and beyond it – stretching to the horizon – lay a rippling green sea of reeds. Like some vast creature it shimmered and swayed. He caught the clamour of waterbirds, the croaking of millions of frogs, and here and there, the restless glimmer of water.

'What can you see?' panted Pirra, coming up behind him. 'Is it . . .' She sucked in her breath.

Far out in the marshes, a pink cloud rose and split apart into hundreds of astonishing birds, like rose-coloured swans, but with weird upside-down beaks. Echo seemed to have forgotten her unease, and was swooping after them and scattering them purely for fun. Then she did an amazing twisting somersault, dived into the reeds, and burst out again in a flurry of terrified ducks.

Watching the falcon's ecstatic rampage, Hylas said to Kem, 'Is this –'

'Yes,' said Kem. 'Ta-Mehi. The Great Green.' He sounded scared.

Havoc had scented water, and was bounding down the ridge. As the three of them followed more slowly, Kem said, 'When we get inside, stay close and keep to the edge. Easy to get lost in there. Things move around.'

'What things?' Pirra said impatiently.

Kem hesitated. 'Papyrus. Waterways. And lotta animals, very –'

'– dangery, yes, we know,' said Pirra.

This side of the ridge was dense with thornscrub. Halfway down, Hylas stopped to dig a thorn out of his heel. By the time he'd reached the bottom, the others had gone on ahead and were out of sight.

In front of him, the sand was no more than twenty paces across, but he didn't like it, it felt too exposed. Beyond it, the Great Green was a creaking wall of reeds, warding him back.

'Pirra?' he whispered. 'Kem? Havoc?' Had they already crossed into the reeds, or were they still on this side, somewhere in the scrub?

Without warning, an antelope galloped past, trailing a red wake of dust. Its ghostly white hide was dark with sweat. It was running for its life.

Hylas dropped behind a bush and drew his knife.

He didn't have to wait long. A pack of dogs went hurtling after the antelope. As they sped past, Hylas took in their coarse red fur and collars of spiked bronze. Hunting dogs. He had time to think, *warriors* – then there they were, a band of half-naked men following their hounds at a disciplined run amid clouds of dust.

They were almost out of sight when the last man

ran back and stooped to examine the sand not ten paces from where Hylas hid.

The warrior was stocky and muscular, and his reddish-brown limbs were ridged with battle-scars. Despite the scorching sand, his feet were bare, and he wore nothing but a kilt of heavy linen, covered by rawhide webbing. His black hair was cut to shoulder-length, with a fringe across the brow. Though he had no beard, his face was as rough as a desert crag, and the charcoal bars daubed beneath his eyes gave him a stony, inhuman look. He carried a longbow and a wovengrass quiver of arrows, a hefty spear and a large curved bronze knife. On a thong about his neck hung five shrivelled human ears.

Hylas felt sick. Something Kem had said came back to him. *They get paid for each kill they can prove.* Hylas pictured the warrior hacking off an ear as proof, then leaving the corpse for the jackals . . .

Someone touched his arm, and he nearly cried out. It was Pirra, her eyes wide and dark.

Together they watched the warrior straighten up and scan his surroundings.

One of his comrades ran back and said something in Egyptian. The first man rapped out one word. His comrade blenched. Together, they ran off to join the others.

'Did you understand any of that?' breathed Hylas when they'd gone.

'Lion,' she whispered. 'They must have found Havoc's tracks.'

Hylas swallowed. 'Will they come after her?'

'I don't think so, only the Perao is allowed to hunt lions.'

'But if they find out we're here, they'll come after us. Where's Kem?'

She tossed her head in disgust. 'Gone!'

'*What?* How?'

'He was ahead of me, he shot across the gap and into the reeds. I was about to follow when the dogs appeared –'

'Well then maybe he didn't know you'd got left behind.'

'Then why didn't he come back? Face it, Hylas, he's gone. It's just as I expected. He led us to a border patrol, then fled.'

Hylas didn't want to believe it, but Kem was certainly gone. Now what to do? Ahead of them, the reeds rustled and creaked, exhaling a swampy, rotten smell. Hylas thought of cobras and crocodiles, and the river horses which Kem had said could bite a man in half.

'We'll have to risk it,' said Pirra in a low voice. 'We can't stay out here, they might come back.'

Hylas gave a reluctant nod.

Cutting off a thorn bough to brush away their tracks, he checked that there was no one in sight. Then, hand in hand, they sped across the sand and plunged into the Great Green.

7

'Hylas, where are you?'

'Over here.'

'Where? I can't –'

'I'm coming.' He squeezed through a clump of stiff green stems, and back to Pirra.

'We need to stay *together*,' she muttered angrily.

'I thought we were, it sounded like you were right behind!'

'Well I wasn't, I was nowhere near!' In the shifting light, her small pointed face had a greenish tinge, and her crinkly black hair clung damply to her shoulders. He thought she looked like a water spirit. A frightened one.

Together, they squelched through the dim green tunnel that snaked through the reeds. It was just after dawn, but stiflingly hot. Midges whined in their ears, damselflies zoomed past. The *eep eep* of frogs reminded Hylas painfully of Issi. Frogs were her favourite animal.

Unseen creatures slithered away from his feet, and everywhere, birds flew up with piercing cries. Herons, swallows, ducks. Some were familiar, yet weirdly coloured, as if in a dream. He saw doves with mean red eyes, and kingfishers that weren't blue, but stripy black and white. He glimpsed a moorhen that was bright *purple*, with scarlet beak and legs.

And always the shifting, groaning reeds. They were taller than any he'd ever seen, with no leaves, only rigid green stems thicker than his wrist, and nodding heads like huge feathery green fans. They creaked and whispered of the intruders in their midst.

'I've never seen reeds this thick,' he said, forcing his way through a clump.

'They're not reeds,' said Pirra. 'They're papyrus. It's sacred. Egyptians make a kind of cloth from the stems. Scribes paint it with spells.'

'Well whatever they're called, they don't like us.'

They heard him. Out of nowhere a wind blew up and the papyrus swayed violently, tightening around him with crushing force. 'Help me with this,' he gasped.

It took both of them to wrench him free.

'Maybe they don't want us to go that way,' panted Pirra. Her hand went to the *wedjat* amulet at her breast.

'But the other way's too far in.'

She nodded. 'We need to go back. Kem said to keep to the edge.'

Hylas noticed that although she was convinced that Kem had abandoned them, she still wanted to follow his advice. Hylas decided not to point this out.

'I can't believe he just left us,' he said.

'I knew he would,' Pirra said in disgust.

Hylas didn't want it to be true. He admired Kem's skill at surviving, and he *liked* him. 'Maybe he got spooked by the border guards, then couldn't find us. Maybe he's looking for us right now.'

Pirra snorted. Then she stopped. 'This isn't right either.'

He nodded. 'We need to backtrack.'

But now they couldn't find the tunnel they'd just left, the papyrus had closed in behind them. *Things move around*, Kem had warned. *Papyrus, waterways . . .*

As soon as they went forwards again, the papyrus made it easy, parting before them, leading them deeper into the Great Green.

In the distance, they heard Havoc's loud, *yowmping* call: *Where are you?* To Hylas' relief, she sounded curious, rather than worried. He imitated her call: *yowm, yowm: I'm here!*

Pirra was scanning what she could see of the sky, for Echo. She shook her head. 'I get the feeling she's far away, enjoying all the birds.' She sounded strained, as if she was trying to give herself courage.

'What's *that*?' hissed Hylas.

From further in came a deep, bellowing *mvu mvu*.

They stared at each other. Hylas remembered Kem's tales of river horses and giant lizards. He prayed that Havoc would have the sense to leave whatever was making that noise well alone.

They came to a narrow stream, like a slow brown snake. Floating on the surface lay enormous round waterlily leaves, with spiky buds jutting through. The buds weren't white, but a fragrant purplish-blue. 'Lotus,' murmured Pirra. 'They're sacred, too.'

Their heady sweetness was making Hylas dizzy. His temples ached. He prayed that he wasn't about to have a vision.

'D'you think the water's safe to drink?' he heard Pirra say.

'I don't think we've got any choice,' he mumbled.

The water was so murky he couldn't see deeper

than a hand's breadth, and it tasted swampy. To his relief, the pain in his head vanished. 'D' you think this is the River?' he said.

Pirra shook her head. 'Userref said it's more than two arrowshots wide.'

He filled the waterskin, and felt the current against his fingers. From what he could see of the Sun, the stream was flowing north. He pointed south. 'We need to go that way.'

'How d'you know?'

'I don't, but sometimes when rivers get near the Sea, they split into lots of little channels. I think that's what this is. If we follow it upstream, we might find the River itself.'

They hadn't gone far when once again they heard Havoc: *Where are you?*

Hylas opened his mouth to reply – then shut it. 'Can you smell smoke?' he whispered.

Pirra nodded. 'Did you hear that? It sounds like – a *donkey*!'

Ahead of them, the papyrus thinned, and became a belt of the kind of reeds Hylas was used to. Peering through, he saw another, wider stream, with muddy red banks and a sandbank in the middle, strewn with logs. Not far from where they hid, a flock of glossy black ibis with long curving beaks was waking up in an acacia tree. Beyond that stood the strangest trees he'd ever seen. Their trunks were criss-crossed like pine cones, and their spiky branches sprang outwards from a single point, like the Sun's rays, with knife-like leaves all pointing down.

'Date-palms,' said Pirra. 'We had one in a pot in the House of the Goddess.'

Hylas didn't reply. On the far side of the stream, smoke was rising from a cluster of mudbrick huts. Again the donkey brayed. A dog barked, geese honked, goats bleated. The familiar sounds of a village waking up.

Three women in white linen shifts appeared and made their way down the bank, bearing waterpots on their heads. Upstream, two fishermen were heading out in a punt that seemed to be made of bundles of papyrus lashed together. One squatted in front, holding a net. The other was pushing off with a pole.

It was all so astonishingly *normal*: the women's earthenware pots, the men's flint knives and woven-grass nets; even the crows and a vulture wheeling over the dungheap . . .

And yet.

Pirra clutched his arm. 'Look at that,' she breathed. The inlet where the women were filling their pots was barred by a line of crossed poles. Was that to keep them in? Or something out?

Then Hylas saw that one of the women was missing her left foot. She hobbled about quite easily on her stump. The fisherman casting his net had only three fingers on one hand. The man holding the pole had a big puckered scar on his calf. Like a bite-mark.

Perhaps sensing that he was being watched, the fisherman turned and scanned the bank.

Hylas and Pirra drew back. They'd seen enough.

For once, the papyrus decided to help, and showed them another tunnel, this one much wider, leading roughly south.

'What kind of creature could have bitten them like that?' whispered Pirra.

Hylas looked at her. He didn't need to say it. They were both thinking of river horses and giant lizards.

As they headed on down the shadowy green tunnel, every creak and rustle became fraught with menace.

Suddenly, Pirra wrinkled her nose in disgust. 'Ugh, what's that *smell*?'

Hylas halted and looked about him. The close-packed papyrus stems that made the tunnel walls were spattered with sticky black dung. He'd never seen or smelt anything like it.

'Hylas?' said Pirra.

The tunnel in the papyrus was so wide they could walk abreast, and it sloped down to where, twenty paces away, he caught a glimmer of water. The ground beneath his feet was crushed papyrus, trodden flat. With a sickening jolt, it came to him: some creature had *trampled* its way through these stiff green stems, and made this tunnel. Something huge.

Early morning is the dangery time, Kem had told him. *All night they feed on the banks, and when the Sun start getting hot-hot, they move down to the water to cool off. Never get between a river horse and the water, it bite you in half . . .*

'We need to get out of this tunnel now,' said Hylas.

'The papyrus is too thick,' Pirra said tautly, 'I can't get through.'

Higher up the tunnel, the tops of the papyrus were swaying violently, although there was no wind. The ground was shaking. The next instant, Hylas saw a great grey boulder filling the tunnel – but it wasn't a boulder, it was a massive snout the colour of wet stone.

He leapt one way, Pirra the other. No time to go after her, it was all he could do to force his way through the close-packed stems and out of the tunnel.

Moments later, the river horses came crashing

down it, a grunting, jostling herd of monsters with snouts as vast as their swollen bellies. They were so close he could have touched them if he'd dared, and they moved at terrifying speed on their stumpy legs. One tried to push past another with an angry bellow, blasting Hylas with swampy breath and revealing an enormous red maw bristling with long yellow tusks.

As suddenly as they'd come, they were gone. He heard a great commotion of splashing as they lumbered into the water – then silence.

He breathed out a long breath. 'That was close.'

Pirra didn't answer.

'Pirra? *Pirra?*'

8

Hylas forced his way back through the papyrus stems and into the tunnel. It was empty. Pirra wasn't there.

Which means she got out in time, Hylas told himself. I went one way, she went the other. Yes, that must be it.

Crossing to the other side of the tunnel, he pushed through the papyrus stems. 'Pirra?' he whispered – unwilling to shout, in case the villagers heard. Or the river horses.

No answer. But the papyrus was so thick that she couldn't have gone far.

As he shouldered his way through, nightmare images flashed through his mind. Pirra seized in the giant red maw of a river horse, dragged underwater, bitten in half . . .

Without realizing it, he'd passed from the papyrus into another stand of reeds. Stems whipped his face. Dead leaves rustled underfoot. He hadn't been among them long when he emerged, blinking, onto a muddy red bank before a dazzle of open water.

He was back at the stream. But that didn't make sense, he'd been going the other way. And yet there was the sandbank and the acacia tree and the date-palms . . .

Although – was it the *same* stream? He could see no sign of the village or the fishermen, and no logs on that sandbank, although several were lying near it, half-submerged, and a few floated not far from where he stood. The date-palms were different, too. Some of them were leaning right over the stream, and beneath them in the shallows, waterlilies rocked gently.

'Pirra, where *are* you?' he cried.

These waterlily buds had burst open into large tri-angular flowers with purple-blue petals as sharp as spears. They jutted upwards, like hands reaching for the Sun, and their scent was overpowering.

In consternation, Hylas cast up and down the bank. If only Pirra would emerge from the reeds, dishevelled and furious with him. Or if Echo would swoop down and help him find her – or Havoc pounce on him in one of her mock ambushes.

But the reeds and the papyrus murmured their secrets to each other. They knew where Pirra was, but they wouldn't tell.

A flock of ducks flew down and landed in the middle of the stream. Distractedly, Hylas watched their wake rippling outwards, stirring a big sunken log floating near the lilies.

Suddenly, lights flashed behind his eyes, and the burning finger stabbed his temples. No no please, not now . . .

Then it was too late, and his senses turned preternaturally sharp as the veil hiding the spirit world blew away. He *saw* the purple scent of waterlilies hazing the air. He heard the tiny suck of frog feet moving among the reeds – and the slow, strong thump of some water monster's swampy heart.

Why couldn't he hear Pirra's?

Again he glanced up and down the banks, but all he saw were reeds and papyrus – a searing green against the throbbing red banks – and his own shadow, stretching blackly behind him, with its hands on its hips.

What? His own arms were hanging by his sides.

He stared over his shoulder. What lay behind him was definitely his shadow. It extended from his feet, as shadows do – *but it wasn't doing what he was doing.*

As he stood frozen in disbelief, his shadow raised one hand and shaded its eyes; then, with its other hand, it pointed at something in the shallows.

Out of the tail of his eye, Hylas saw another duck gliding in to land. With his heightened senses, its blue and yellow plumage glowed unbearably bright, and its landing splash was a waterfall roar.

His shadow was watching it too. Both its hands were back on its hips, and its head was cocked, as if it was waiting for something to happen.

Arching its neck, the duck gave itself a vigorous shake and folded its wings. Behind it, the waterlilies exploded. The duck didn't even have time to squawk. Giant jaws engulfed it with a crunching snap and dragged it down.

The giant lizard swallowed the duck in two
chomping gulps, then turned with a snakelike twist and swam towards Hylas.

Crocodile, he thought numbly. This is a crocodile.

It was a monster not of flesh, but of stone. Its massive armoured body bristled with spikes. Its teeth
jutted the length of its scaly jaws, which it held agape
in a meaningless grin – and its empty yellow stare was
fixed on him.

Slowly, he backed away.

The crocodile floated in the shallows, watching him.

His mind darted in panic. Lizards move fast, he
would never outrun it, and his knife would never
pierce that flinty hide.

With another horrible snakelike twist, the monster

came scything through the waterlilies towards him. At the same moment, he heard rustling *behind* him, and a *second* crocodile burst from the reeds, moving at incredible speed on its bent lizard legs.

There was only one thing to do. Hylas raced for the nearest date-palm.

Its trunk grew at a slant over the water, he managed to scramble a short way up. Not far enough. Both crocodiles were closing fast. The trunk had no branches to grab on to, they were all clustered at the crown, high overhead. He'd have to try something he'd only done once before, years ago, when a boar had chased him up a pine tree.

Clasping the trunk between his legs and clinging on with one arm, he yanked the coil of rope over his head, then wound one end round his right wrist, passed the rope behind the trunk, and twisted it frantically around his left wrist, so that he was gripping the trunk in a tight rope sling. The tree's bark had that weird pine-cone roughness, made of lots of scratchy little ledges, and the rawhide snagged, as he'd prayed it would. He jerked it higher. Then, gripping with both feet, he half-hopped, half-hoisted himself up.

It didn't take him far. With appalling agility, the crocodile from the reeds leapt at him with jaws agape. It came so close that he caught a blast of foetid breath.

It fell back, then tried again. Grimly, Hylas struggled higher: shuffle, hop, hoist.

The crocodile gaped with that ghastly grin, but made no further attempt. Relief washed over him. It didn't look as if crocodiles could climb trees.

Far above him, the Sun flashed through the spiky branches clustered at the crown. He risked a glance down – and saw with a jolt that he was now right over the water.

Behind him on the bank, the smaller crocodile, the one from the reeds, seemed to have lost interest in its troublesome prey. Slithering down the bank, it swam towards the sandbank, where more crocodiles were now hauling themselves out to bask in the Sun.

But the big one from the shallows had climbed the bank, and was lying beneath his date-palm. On land, it was even more enormous than it had been in the water. From snout to tailtip, it was longer than three tall men laid head to foot, and its scaly belly could have swallowed a deer.

As Hylas watched, it turned and slid back into the water, and went under. He strained to make it out, but its swampy hide had vanished uncannily into the shallows.

He waited. Something told him it hadn't gone away.

He was thirsty. Only now did he realize that he'd

lost the waterskin. He must have dropped it in the river-horse tunnel. Pirra would be furious. He held on to that.

Below him, the shallows were quiet. The waterlilies had stopped rocking. Had the crocodile gone back to the sandbank?

The lilies erupted, giant jaws clashing a hand's-breadth from his face. With a cry he recoiled, nearly losing his grip on the rope. The crocodile fell back with a drenching splash.

The waterlilies rocked. The wind hissed through the reeds. A dove uttered a rippling coo that sounded a lot like laughter.

The rope was biting into his hands and wrists. He scarcely felt it. He waited for the monster to come again.

At the edge of a lilypad, two pebbles silently broke the surface – and peeled open to reveal the stony yellow crocodile stare. The pupils were black slits. Hylas couldn't look away. He was falling into them . . .

Just in time, he wrenched his gaze away.

His arms were beginning to shake. He couldn't hold on for much longer. Forcing himself to ignore the monster, he shifted the rope higher up the trunk, and resumed his climb. He had to reach the branches at the top.

He could feel the crocodile watching.

Crocodile, Kem had told him, *run fast as a horse on land, and hold his breath underwater for half a day. He smell the scent of a child at forty paces, he hear it blink . . . Egyptians call him He Who Watches What He Would Seize.*

Hylas glanced down.

It was still watching. Implacable, totally without feeling.

Deep within Hylas, his spirit rallied. 'Well, you're not going to get me,' he gasped through clenched teeth. 'If I fall out of this tree, I swear I'll stick in your throat and choke you to death – I'll cut my way out of your belly if I have to . . .'

With one supreme effort, he hauled himself into the crown of the date-palm. Not much room among the big clusters of knobbly brown fruit, and the stiff, dagger-sharp branches. 'See?' he panted at the crocodile. 'I'm not finished yet!'

'I'm not finished yet!' he yelled. Birds flew up from the reeds in a clatter of wings and startled squawks. Hylas was shaking uncontrollably. The crocodile was still watching.

A branch snapped off from the date-palm and dropped on to the lilypads.

The crocodile didn't stir. No creature Hylas had ever encountered was so utterly without response.

He couldn't bear it. He had to make it *do* something. Awkwardly shifting position, he took a pebble from the pouch at his belt and threw it as hard as he could at the monster's head.

His aim was off, he hit a lilypad with a splash. His next was better, it struck the flinty hide with a thud and bounced off with another splash. The crocodile didn't even blink. Hylas didn't throw another.

The Sun rose higher. He tensed and untensed his legs, to stop them going numb. His head was throbbing; the palm's branches gave little shade. He thought with longing of the waterskin.

The crocodile went on watching.

It's a messy way to die, in a crocodile's jaws, Kem had said. *He drag you under, then roll you round and round till you drown; they call it the death roll. Or sometime, he just thrash you from side to side, till you're all tore to bits . . .*

On the sandbank in midstream, some of the crocodiles had woken up. Squinting through the branches, Hylas watched first one, then another, slither into the water with that dreadful snakelike ease and come gliding towards him.

Too late, he remembered something else Kem had said. *Any splash, any stir in the water, it draw the crocodile. He can feel the flick of a fish's fin, the touch of a deer's muzzle brush the surface as it drinks . . .*

86

I shouldn't have thrown those pebbles, thought Hylas.

The crocodiles were beneath him now: some in the water, some hauling themselves up on to the bank. They would wait all day and all night until he dropped from the tree like a ripe fruit.

He wouldn't stand a chance. He wouldn't even have time to scream.

IO

Pirra felt a cry rising in her throat, and choked it down. 'Hylas where *are* you?' she hissed.

She'd thought he was behind her, but by the time the river horses had gone crashing through the tunnel, she'd realized he wasn't, and she was lost.

It was terrifying being alone in the Great Green. She longed for Havoc or Echo, but she'd heard no more calls from Havoc, and she knew that Echo was far away. Sometimes, when the falcon was flying, Pirra felt that she was flying too. Now she had a fleeting impression of rushing wind, ducks exploding from glittering water and the fierce exhilaration of the hunt, driving all else from the falcon's mind . . .

A desperate shout dragged her back to herself.

Horror washed over her. That was Hylas. He was too far away to make out the words, but there was no mistaking his anger and fear. And it took a lot to frighten Hylas.

Starting towards where she guessed his cry had come from, Pirra burst through the papyrus on to a muddy bank rustling with reeds. A hot wind lifted her hair. A snake flickered down a hole. Before her lay another stream, much wider than before.

Another shout from Hylas. Then nothing. It sounded as if he was on the other side, further downstream.

Pirra skittered down the bank and eyed the murky green water. It looked deep, but she could swim, and if she had to, she could rest on that sandbank in the middle.

She was about to wade in when, upstream, she spotted the humped grey bulk of river horses. One gave a cavernous yawn and bared its big yellow tusks. Another surfaced with a *whoosh*, alarmingly close. Snorting and spouting water, it waggled its small round ears and glared at her with bulging, frog-like eyes.

Pirra backed away. At her feet, a long shallow groove led down to the water's edge. On either side of it she made out the prints of large clawed feet. She pictured the crocodile slithering down the mud, into the shallows. She scrambled up the bank.

Now what to do? She couldn't swim across, not even for Hylas.

If in doubt, make an offering: get the spirits on your side. She'd forgotten to do that when they'd entered the Great Green, maybe that was why things had gone wrong.

Her last remaining necklace from the House of the Goddess was under her tunic, tied around her waist: a string of amethyst beads hung with small gold poppyheads. Reaching under her skirt, she snapped off a poppyhead. 'Spirits of the Great Green,' she muttered, 'help me find Hylas and keep him safe!'

She cast the gold into the water and watched its glinting descent. A large fish rose from the murk and swallowed it in one gulp. Was that good or bad?

She started along the bank, heading downstream. Perhaps she would come across a bridge, or even a fisherman willing to help her find Hylas, for a price.

A bird flew up at her feet, its frantic wings brushing her face. She was so startled she nearly ran right past the boat.

It was small and made of bunches of papyrus tied together. Its owner hadn't bothered to moor it, he'd simply jammed it among the reeds.

Pirra had never handled a boat in her life, but she didn't give herself time to worry. Hauling it free of the reeds, she jumped in. It rocked violently, water sloshing over the sides.

She couldn't find a paddle, only a pole floating alongside. She remembered the fisherman pushing off from the bank, and did what he'd done, raising the pole with both hands and jamming it into the mud, then pushing with all her might.

The pole stuck fast and the boat shot forwards, nearly leaving her in the mud. Somehow, she managed to haul both boat and pole back together. This time, she didn't jab too hard, and when the boat glided clear, she managed to stay with it and yank the pole free.

The current was strong, and the boat sat alarmingly low in the water. She felt horribly exposed: at any moment, an outraged fisherman might spot her from the bank.

Something bumped against the back of the boat. Pirra's belly turned over. The crocodile flexed its snaky length and swam towards her. She saw its warty snout and the mottled bumps of its eyes; the long armoured ridges down its back. Clutching the pole, she bashed it on the nose. It sank without a ripple and disappeared.

Panting, Pirra cast about. Where had it gone? She remembered something Kem had said. *It's the crocodile you* don't *see that gets you.*

Muttering a prayer to the Goddess, she headed off as fast as she could. The opposite bank drew steadily closer. Among the reeds, she spotted movement: was that *Havoc* in there, crouching down?

Suddenly the boat juddered, nearly flinging her out. She'd hit a rock. No, not a rock, a river horse, a young one rearing up, squealing in fright. Desperately, Pirra tried to back away. A giant wave crashed over her, swamping the boat – and *another* river horse surfaced with a furious bellow.

This was no young one. This was the mother.

The lion cub was so famished she'd hardly seen the girl on her bundle of reeds as she'd gone charging into the wet after the baby river pig – but now the *mother* was bursting out at her.

For something so fat, the mother moved terrifyingly fast, surging right past the girl and lunging at the cub. The cub dodged. The river pig's tusks clashed a whisker from her ear. The cub sped up the bank – and swerved to avoid *another* river pig lumbering towards her.

Instead of attacking her, this one spun round and

waggled its enormous bottom, lashed its stubby little tail, and spattered her with stinky black dung.

Filthy and furious, the lion cub fled.

To think that at first, she'd actually *liked* this soggy new place. It had been such a relief after the burning lands to have enough to drink, and she'd always loved splashing about in the wet. She'd had fun chasing ducks, and had even found some delicious crunchy fish, conveniently trapped in one of those little grass sacks which humans used for catching them.

But the reeds were swarming with midges and ticks, so many ticks. Soon her pelt was crawling with them: biting, itching, driving her mad, especially the ones in her scruff, that she couldn't lick off.

Then she'd lost the scent of the boy and the girl. She'd heard him calling, but she couldn't *find* him.

And now all this dung. Licking her forepaw, she rubbed her muzzle to clean it off. When she did it again, it tasted so awful that she gave up.

Miserably, she found a patch of wet where there didn't seem to be any river pigs, and waded in. The mud squelched soothingly beneath her paws. She stuck her head in the wet and washed off the dung, and felt a bit better.

At that moment, she caught the boy's scent. At last!

Bounding up the bank to catch the wind, she smelt that he was somewhere behind that little island in the middle. Eagerly, she leapt back into the wet and started swimming as fast as she could.

━━●━━

The falcon liked this strange new place – it was *much* better than the burning lands. There was plenty of wet for bathing, and those huge grey monsters in the shallows made excellent perches.

And so many birds! She'd eaten a duck, and had fun scaring those stripy kingfishers that were ridiculously easy to catch, although they tasted *horrible*. She'd even crunched up a few little blue damselflies, because they moved so slowly it seemed a pity not to.

It was such a shame that neither her humans nor the lion cub seemed to like this place. Just now, she'd seen the girl gliding very fast over the wet on her bunch of reeds. The falcon had sensed that the girl was frightened, but had no idea how to help; and she kept getting distracted by all the birds.

The lion cub wasn't doing well, either. She'd just been chased by one of the grey monsters. She'd scrambled out of the wet and shot up a tree, and the falcon had been impressed. The cub wasn't usually good at climbing trees.

A few wingbeats away, the falcon came upon the

boy – and he, too, was up a tree. The falcon was puzzled. Why was everyone climbing trees?

Hylas was getting desperate. He was dizzy with thirst, and he'd been crouching for so long that his legs had gone numb. Sooner or later, he was going to fall out of this tree.

Around him, life was going on as usual. Birds chirped, frogs *eep-eep*ed and a crow on the bank held down a snailshell with one foot and tugged out the squidgy mollusc with its beak.

The Sun was getting low. Beneath him, the waterlilies had closed their petals and were slowly sinking below the surface. Somewhere upstream, a herd of river horses was uttering deep *mvu mvu*s.

And still the crocodiles waited. Some had gone, others had come, but the biggest, the one that had attacked him first, had never stirred from the waterlilies. Only its nostrils and eyebumps showed, but he knew it was there. He felt its stare.

Twice, he'd dozed off and nearly fallen in. After that, he'd tied himself to the crown of the date-palm. But its branches were alarmingly brittle, and he dreaded the whole thing snapping and taking him with it, into the jaws of the monster.

He thought of Pirra and Echo and Havoc, lost in

the Great Green. He thought of Issi, far away across the Sea in Messenia. And here he was, stuck up a tree. Was this how it was going to end?

He was jolted awake by a tremendous splash. Out in midstream, two river horses were fighting, bellowing with massive jaws agape and lashing out with their tusks. The others in the herd parted to let them through, and the pair went crashing in and out of the water, gouging bloody furrows in each other's flanks.

They were moving towards Hylas, and below him, some of the crocodiles were swimming away. His hopes rose.

But the big crocodile remained beneath the date-palm. It wasn't going anywhere.

At last, one river horse proved the stronger, and the other one fled. Champing the water, the victor bellowed its triumph: *I've won! I am the strongest!*

Its huge rump bumped against the crocodile, which swung round with half-open jaws. The river horse turned on the crocodile with an irritable grunt: *I'm not afraid of you!*

Hylas willed them to fight, but the big crocodile merely drifted sideways, while the river horse just snorted and waggled its ears.

Hylas glanced from the river horse to the crocodile.

He drew his slingshot from his belt. Maybe he could help things along.

Parting the date-palm's branches for a better shot, he loaded his slingshot and let fly. A child of five could have hit the river horse, and his pebble struck it smack on the snout. It merely twitched its ears and glared at the crocodile.

Hylas pelted the river horse again and again. When the pebbles ran out, he used the date-palm's hard brown fruit. All he achieved were angry snorts.

Then a lucky shot got it in the eye. That did it. With an outraged bellow, the river horse went for the crocodile. The crocodile fought back. Thrashing and rolling in a chaos of white water, the two monsters crashed against Hylas' date-palm, shaking the tree and nearly pitching him out. The crocodile clamped its jaws on the river horse's snout. The river horse squealed and reared out of the water. With one jerk of its massive head, it tore itself free of the crocodile's grip and flung the monster out into midstream. With astonishing speed, the river horse went after the crocodile, grabbed its belly in its vast maw – and chomped it in two.

Waves sloshed up and down the banks, rocking the shredded remains of the waterlilies.

Hylas had to act fast. It wouldn't be long before the other crocodiles returned. Shakily, he untied the rope that bound him to the date-palm, and pounded the feeling back into his legs.

A short while later, as he made his way down, he glimpsed something nosing towards him over the water. He nearly fell out of the tree.

Pirra sat in a punt with Havoc crouched uneasily before her. Both were muddy, bedraggled, and staring up at him.

'What are you doing up there?' said Pirra.

11

The falcon checked her perch for ants, and finding none, half-spread her wings to catch the cooling Wind. Her tree was peaceful and safe, and she liked the noise of her earthbound companions lumbering about below.

They too had found a safe roost, a good distance from the tunnels of the big grey monsters, and from the wet where the giant lizards lurked. The boy and girl were crunching up a pair of ducks they'd killed and burnt, and the lion cub, having demolished her share, was busy licking ticks off her pelt. She couldn't reach the ones at the back of her neck, so the falcon flew down and perched on her shoulder and did it for her. The falcon liked the taste of the ticks bursting in her beak, and the cub enjoyed it too, tilting her head so that the falcon could do under her ears.

When the falcon had had enough ticks, she flew back to her branch, tucked one leg under her belly, and settled to roost.

She loved this strange, rustly place. She only wished the others loved it too.

The Great Green rang with the calls of millions of frogs. The fire hissed and sent sparks shooting into the dark.

'D'you want the last wing?' said Pirra with her mouth full.

'You have it,' said Hylas without looking up.

'There's some skin left, and a bit of reed root.'

He shook his head. He was plaiting two large nets out of reeds, and planned to sling them between pairs of date-palms, so that they could sleep clear of the ground.

'What's bothering you?' said Pirra. 'Is it the fact that *I* rescued *you*, and not the other way around?'

'Of course not. Anyway, you didn't rescue me.'

'Yes I did.'

'No you didn't, I'd already got rid of the crocodiles.'

'You sound like Kem, trying to prove he's not a coward.'

Hylas sighed. 'I wish we knew where he was. And you don't understand, it's *important* for him to prove himself.'

Pirra snorted. 'Why?'

'He told me that in his tribe, for a boy to become a man, he has to prove his bravery. He's supposed to slip into Egypt and steal a weapon from a warrior. It's how he got caught and taken for a slave.'

'Well it sounds daft to me,' said Pirra.

'You're not a boy, it's different for you.' But Hylas understood Kem's need to prove himself, as he felt it, too. His own father had been a coward, who'd refused to fight the Crows. And because of that, Akastos, the man whom Hylas admired above all others, had had to leave his farm and wander for years in exile. Hylas longed to make amends to Akastos. He longed to wipe out the stain of his father's cowardice.

'So what's bothering you?' said Pirra, slitting the reed root with her knife and frowning at it.

'Nothing,' lied Hylas.

She made a face, and gnawed the sweet, sticky root. 'You keep rubbing your temple. Have you had another vision?'

'No!' he snapped. Sometimes, Pirra noticed too much. And he didn't want to talk about what he'd seen just before the crocodile attacked. In the beginning, his visions had been fleeting corner-of-the-eye glimpses of ghosts. Later, in the House of the Goddess, they'd been more distinct. And now . . . He'd seen his shadow moving by itself. It had been so clear. Were the visions getting stronger?

That frightened him more than river horses or crocodiles, because he didn't know where it would end. And it seemed to put a wall between him and Pirra. How could he protect her when he didn't know what was happening to himself?

Havoc flopped over and clouted him with one fore-paw, then rolled on to her back and lay inelegantly with all four paws flopping outwards.

Hylas scratched her belly and picked off a tick. 'She doesn't realize she's nearly full-grown,' he remarked. 'You need to grow up, Havoc. I can't look after you for ever.'

Havoc rumbled contentedly and gazed at him through slitted eyes as he raked her fur for more ticks. Pirra asked what he was doing, and he held one up for her to see. It was the size of his little fingernail, and swollen with blood.

'Yuk,' she said.

'You've got one on your leg.'

'*What*? Where?'

'Behind your knee. Hold still, I'll pinch it off.'

The skin behind her knee was pale gold and incredibly soft. Touching it made him dizzy and hot. 'There,' he muttered, tossing the tick in the fire.

A tiny bead of blood welled up where the tick had been and Pirra rubbed it away with her finger. 'Thanks,' she said quietly. In the firelight, her face was high-boned and handsome. Her eyebrows reminded Hylas of two little wings, and her bright eyes met his without blinking.

Jumping to his feet, he grabbed one of the nets, then lashed it to the trunk of a date-palm at head-height and gave the knot a vicious tug. 'Time we got some sleep,' he said angrily.

Pirra cleaned her knife on her tunic and looked at Hylas, who was tying the other end of the net to a tree. His tawny mane hung in his eyes, and the firelight caught the golden hairs along his jaw. He was scowling. She could see a muscle twitching in his cheek.

She knew what was wrong. Most of the time, they were exactly as they'd always been: sometimes squabbling, sometimes doubled up with laughter, sometimes silent in the way that only best friends can be. Then one of them would glance at the other, and there'd be this heat crackling between them, like the air before a storm.

They were both fourteen summers old. They couldn't go on being just friends for much longer. People didn't, they became mated pairs. Hylas knew this as well as she did. What was holding him back?

On Keftiu, she'd been pretty sure it was because she was highborn and he wasn't. But these days, she was no longer the daughter of the High Priestess, she was just a girl with a scar – so it couldn't be that.

A girl with a scar . . .

Havoc ambled over and gave her a rasping lick on the cheek. Pushing the young lioness aside, Pirra touched the mark on her face.

She'd been twelve when she'd done it. At the time, she'd been proud, it made her look different. Now she hated it. She'd tried everything to make it fade, but nothing had worked. Was this what was coming between her and Hylas? Her scar?

Havoc went to Hylas and rubbed against his thigh, and he twisted another tick off her ear and tossed it high, and she leapt and snapped it up in mid-air.

Despite herself, Pirra chuckled.

Hylas' lip curled. 'We'd better get some sleep,' he repeated. But this time, he didn't sound angry.

Pirra eyed the two nets slung between pairs of date-palms. 'You really think we can sleep in those things?'

'Well, you're welcome to lie on the ground with all the snakes and the scorpions.'

'What about ticks? Will we be avoiding them too?'

'Oh, yes.'

She shot him a doubtful glance. 'Are you just saying that?'

'Oh, yes.'

She chucked a duck bone at him and he laughed and chucked it back, and things were all right again between them.

Pirra's sling was scratchy, and sagged so much that she was almost doubled up inside it. As she wriggled about trying to get comfortable, she realized with a jolt what she was missing. With a cry, she jumped to the ground.

Hylas was beside her in an instant with his knife in his fist. 'What's wrong?'

'My *wedjat*!'

'What?'

'My *amulet*! The Eye of Heru, the one Userref gave me! Oh, Hylas, it's *gone*!'

'When did you have it last? Before or after you found me in the tree?' Hylas stifled a yawn, and hoped Pirra didn't notice.

She was far too upset to notice anything. 'Um – after,

I think. Yes, I'm sure, the thong kept coming loose –
but I *fixed* it!'

'It's good that it was after, we can retrace our steps
tomorrow. We'll find it, Pirra. It must've got snagged
on something and fallen off.'

'*Tomorrow?*' She was aghast. 'But anything could've
happened to it by then!'

'Well I'm not floundering around in a swamp in the
dark, with river horses and crocodiles and who knows
what else!'

'Hylas, please, we have to find it tonight!' She was
wringing her hands, and there was a pleading note in
her voice which wasn't like her. Pirra never pleaded.

With a sigh, he cut a length of papyrus stem and lit
one end in the embers, then jammed his knife in its
sheath. 'You stay here – I'll take a look. But I'm not
going far. If I don't find it soon, we wait till dawn!'

He hadn't gone ten paces when he realized it was
hopeless. It was much too dark, and his feeble light
only made it harder to see.

But as he headed back to camp, he caught a glint
of bronze in a shaft of moonlight – and there was the
amulet, dangling from a papyrus stem not five paces
away.

He was about to retrieve it when a man emerged
from the shadows and moved towards it.

Hylas swayed as lights flashed behind his eyes and the burning finger stabbed his temple. He dragged his hand to the knife at his hip, but couldn't grab the hilt, his fingers wouldn't obey. And deep in his spirit, he knew that against the being who stood before him in the moonlight, no weapon would be of use.

It had the form of a tall man with broad shoulders and a narrow waist. It wore a kilt of pleated white linen with a green sash knotted at the waist, and on its naked chest, a broad gold collar set with blue and red stones. Its black hair was long, with a fringe across the brow, and its face had a dreadful shimmering brilliance, like the night wind turned to gold.

This is a god, thought Hylas.

It hurt to look. He *must* not look. To see the face of a god is something no mortal can survive.

With a supreme effort, Hylas wrenched his gaze away. But then, from the corner of his eye, he saw the shimmering head begin to change. The ears grew tall and sharp, the face narrowed and stretched – and became the long black pointed muzzle of a jackal.

Not possible, thought Hylas.

But anything is possible for an immortal.

The jackal-headed god bent over the *wedjat* amulet – and seemed to sniff the bronze. Then it drew back, and rose to an appalling height, towering over the very tops of the papyrus – and turned its terrible bright gaze on Hylas.

He felt his spirit shrivel inside him. His arm was heavy as a log as he shielded his eyes and staggered backwards into the reeds.

A sharp pain pierced his ankle. With a cry he glanced down and glimpsed something small scuttling off into the dark.

He fell to his knees. His ankle was burning.

The jackal god was gone. Now Pirra was bending over him. In one hand she clutched a length of burning papyrus, in the other, her *wedjat* amulet. 'Hylas? What's wrong?'

He couldn't speak for the pain, worse than anything he'd known: clawing, scorching, shooting like lightning up his leg.

'Hylas!'

'Scorpion,' he gasped.

12

'A scorpion,' Pirra said in disbelief.

Hylas was baring his teeth and fumbling for his knife. 'Cut it open, suck out the poison!'

'Where did it sting you?'

'Ankle,' he panted.

'We've got to get you back to camp –'

'No, do it now!'

'It's too dark out here, I might cripple you!'

Somehow, she dragged him back to the fire. Havoc stared at them with her ears back. Echo flapped her wings and gaped in alarm.

Hylas collapsed, clutching his leg and taking great heaving gulps of air. The sting was just behind the ankle bone, a small red dot ringed with white. Pirra drew her knife. Her hand shook. She couldn't do it. Hylas grabbed the knife and jabbed it into the wound. In the moonlight, his blood ran black. Pirra bent and sucked the wound, and spat, again and again.

A dark hand seized her arm. 'What bit him?' cried Kem.

With a snarl she twisted out of his grip. '*You!* What are you doing here?'

'*What bit him?*'

'Scorpion. You get away from him!'

'Was it green or black? Did you see?'

When she didn't reply, Kem took Hylas by the shoulders and shook him. 'Hylas! The scorpion! Green or black?' But Hylas only moaned.

Pirra touched his cheek. 'He's burning up.'

Hylas gripped her wrist so hard that she nearly cried out. '*I saw it,*' he whispered, staring up at her with unseeing eyes. 'It was like a man but the air was on fire – it had the head of a *jackal* . . .'

She went cold. The jackal god Anpu was Lord of the Dead. She turned to Kem. 'Can you save him?'

He looked at her. 'No. From this I can't save him.'

She blinked. Then she bent over Hylas. 'I will not let you die,' she said fiercely. 'Kem, we've got to get him to a village. They'll have a wisewoman, or a healer.'

'A *village*?' cried Kem. 'You mad? They'd kill us!'

She hooked her arms under Hylas' arms. 'Help me carry him, it's not far to the boat –'

'*Listen* to me! To Egyptians, you're just barbarians and I'm a runaway slave!'

'A village is his only chance! You will help me get him there. I will not let him die!'

'Are you hearing me? I told you –'

'Just do it. I'll see to the rest.'

He is floating on a Sea of poison. His eyes are full of light, the glare is blinding. It is the jackal god, coming to take him away. Pirra is grasping his hand. He clings to her. She will keep him from being taken.

The jackal god comes closer. Hylas tries to cry out, but he can't speak. Helplessly, he gazes into the blazing fire.

Now he is lying on hard earth. Pirra is still holding his hand. Someone is binding his leg. He tries to kick, but he can't move. The binding on his ankle is painted with tiny weird pictures: a vulture, a wasp. They are twitching, coming alive . . .

Someone pushes his neck on to a block. He struggles, are they going to chop off his head? A rough hand holds him down. Another forces sludge between his lips. 'Drink,' says a voice. 'You will be worse, then better.'

He retches, spewing up his guts. The world is spinning, nothing makes sense. He sees a bird with black eye-stripes, like an Egyptian. A lion the size of a hare, staring at him with luminous green eyes.

A girl bends over him. It isn't Pirra, it's *Issi*. In disbelief he gazes up into his sister's sharp little face. She is scowling at him. 'This is just *like* you, Hylas,' she complains. 'You're always telling *me* to watch my step in the reeds, and now *you* go and get yourself stung!'

'Issi . . . You're *alive*!'

'Of course I'm alive, it's you we're worried about. What were you *thinking*, stumbling around in the dark?'

'You're alive . . .'

He wakes to the night song of frogs. Issi is gone. Havoc is a furry weight against his back. Her deep slow breathing rumbles through him. For a moment he is at peace.

Then the whirling sickness pulls him under.

Hylas drifted awake. Havoc was gone. He was in a thatched lean-to, lying on his side on a wovengrass mat, still with his neck on that wooden block.

A child was kneeling beside him. It wasn't Issi. The sense of loss was overwhelming.

This child was younger, about eight summers, and naked except for a string of green beads about her waist. She had a beaky red nose and red-rimmed eyes, and was painfully thin. She was also bald. Even her eyebrows had been scraped off. Hylas wasn't sure if she was human.

A man appeared behind her. He had the same beaky nose, and wore a bizarre red wig that seemed to be made of palm leaves. The wig was slightly crooked.

Scowling at Hylas, the man barked in Egyptian and forced him to drink from a clay pot. It was sour grey sludge. Hylas spluttered. Darkness bloomed.

When he woke again, cattle were lowing and geese honking. He tried to get up, but couldn't move his limbs. He smelt dung fires and baking bread. I'm in a village, he thought hazily.

His leg no longer hurt, it was violently itchy and swathed in ragged bandages crusted with brownish salt and painted with those weird little signs: a vulture, a wasp . . .

'Don't scratch,' said a familiar voice. 'That's *hes-men*, the sacred salt.' A snort of laughter. 'I know about that, remember? Five years in the mines, digging it up.'

Hylas opened his eyes. '*Kem!*' he croaked.

The black boy gave an uncertain grin. 'How you feel?'

Hylas tried to smile, but the effort was too great. 'Where's Pirra?'

'Asleep. She stayed with you all day, all night. Wouldn't leave till you were outta danger.'

Hylas shut his eyes. 'Glad you back,' he mumbled. 'Didn't think you'd deserted us.'

'Pirra did.' Kem paused. 'When the border guards came, I thought you were hiding on the ridge and Pirra follow me into the Great Green. When they gone, I find no Pirra. I go back up the ridge. Can't find you there or in the Great Green. That for true, Hylas.'

Hylas wanted to tell Kem he believed him, but he didn't have the strength. He lay watching a beetle crawl backwards over the ground, pushing a ball of dung with its hind legs. Through the doorway, tiny green birds flitted about in an acacia tree. They had black eye-stripes, like Egyptians.

'Bee-eaters,' said Kem.

Is that what they are, thought Hylas. 'How'd I get here?' he asked Kem.

Kem told him how he and Pirra had spent most of the night trying to find a village, and about the villagers fending them off with sickles and spears, until Pirra had *made* them take Hylas to their healer.

'That girl!' Kem shook his head in grudging admiration. 'It don't matter she ragged and muddy, she just *order* them, like she a priestess! She whistle to Havoc and tell those villagers, Look at this boy with hair like the Sun, he guarded by a *lion*, creature of great goddess Sekhmet! Then she call down Echo from the sky and tell them, Look at *me*, I got falcon of Ieru on my arm, and mark of the Moon on my face!'

'Clever,' mumbled Hylas.

'For true. And me? Ha! So they don't think me runaway, she tell them I'm *her* slave! Oh, she enjoy that, ordering me about!'

This time, Hylas did manage a smile.

When he looked again, Kem was gone and Pirra was kneeling beside him. There were dark shadows under her eyes. She looked exhausted and tense. 'How do you feel?' she said shakily.

He wanted to tell her that by holding his hand, she'd kept him alive, but he didn't have the strength. 'Weak,' he said. 'I don't like this block under my neck.'

She gave him a tremulous smile. 'It's a headrest, they all sleep on them. If I take it away, they'll only put it back.'

The villagers had given her a coarse linen shift fastened by two straps at the shoulders. With her crinkly black hair and the *wedjat* on her breast, she could be

Egyptian – if it weren't for her pallor, and the leather cuff on her forearm. Hylas thought she looked good, but when she caught him watching, she flicked her hair across her cheek to hide her scar.

'I saw a miniature lion,' he said. 'Didn't you once tell me about miniature lions?'

'It's a cat. The Egyptian name is *myu*.'

'Ah.' He paused. 'Where's Kem?'

'With Havoc. The villagers are terrified of her, that's why they put you here, away from the houses. They've penned all the cattle and what they call "small cattle" – that's sheep and goats and pigs – and shut up the dogs and cats. They've given Havoc so much to eat that she's gone to sleep it off.' She was talking too much, and picking at the frayed edge of the mat.

His leg was itching again. With an enormous effort, he moved his other foot to rub it.

'Don't,' said Pirra, 'it's doing you good.'

'What's this stuff on it?'

'*Hesmen*, beer and river-horse dung. And they dipped in my amulet, they said the god Heru was cured of a scorpion sting, so the *wedjat* has healing power.'

'Who's they? There was a man and a bald child . . .'

'That's Itineb – he's the *sunu*, the healer. His little

daughter is Kawi. She's refusing to eat, he's really worried about her.'

'Itineb. He doesn't like me.'

'He doesn't want us here. He's been even worse to Kem, they all are, because he's a slave.' She paused. 'He keeps telling me he didn't abandon us. It really bothers him.'

Hylas squinted at the binding on his ankle. 'What are those little marks?'

'That's writing. They call it *medu netjer*. Sacred signs.'

'Look like squiggles to me.'

'Writing has power, Hylas, it makes things real. That's a spell to drive away demons. It . . .' She broke off, twisting her hands. 'That writing kept you alive,' she said shakily.

To his horror, he saw that her eyes glittered with tears.

'You could have died!' she blurted out. 'Your heart was going so fast Itineb said it might burst! It was *horrible*!'

All through the endless night, Pirra had sat by his side and faced the unthinkable: that by morning, he might be dead. She couldn't imagine life without Hylas. When she tried, all she saw was darkness.

The night around them had been full of whispers. Once, Havoc had started to her feet, her great golden eyes following something moving outside the shelter: something Pirra couldn't see. She'd sensed that it was the jackal god Anpu. Pacing, waiting to take Hylas.

Then he too had started up, shouting, 'Not yet!' He'd slumped back again, gripping her wrist, as if she alone could keep him from being dragged away.

As dawn broke, Itineb had declared him out of danger, and sent her to his house to sleep. Now she was back, and Hylas lay with his eyes shut and that dreadful blue tinge about the lips. She'd never seen him so weak. She hated it.

Itineb appeared in the doorway and glared at them, then knelt beside Hylas. Close up, his palm-leaf wig looked even more bizarre. Pirra thought it must be scratchy. Maybe that was why it was always on crooked.

Itineb put two fingers to Hylas' wrist, then his throat. 'The voice of the heart is stronger,' he said coldly. 'Tomorrow he can go.'

Pirra was aghast. 'He can't go anywhere, he can't even sit up.'

'He will have to.'

'But –'

'I cannot care for him any longer,' snapped Itineb. 'This is our busiest time: getting the harvest, making ready for the *heb*. And I have a sick child who refuses to eat.'

'How come you speak Akean?' said Hylas.

Itineb ignored him and started changing the bandage.

Hylas stared at the healer's left hand, which ended in a neat, smooth stump. Itineb used it as deftly as if it had been sound.

'A crocodile bit it off,' said the healer, as if Hylas had asked aloud. 'It was a long time ago and no it doesn't hurt.' He spoke wearily, as if he'd been asked many times before.

'Why won't you let us stay for a few more days?' said Pirra. 'I've told you I can pay you gold –'

'I don't want your gold – I want you gone!' Itineb pointed at Hylas' Crow tattoo.

Hylas and Pirra exchanged glances. 'You've seen this mark before,' said Pirra.

'I'm not a Crow,' said Hylas. 'I was their slave and they put their mark on me.'

Itineb snorted. 'You're one of them. In your fever you said the name Userref.'

'Because we're looking for him,' said Pirra. 'He's in a place called Pa-Sobek –'

'– and this proves you are Crows,' retorted Itineb. '*They* seek this man Userref; *they* seek Pa-Sobek!'

'How many?' said Pirra. 'How long ago?'

'A big ship, forty men, led by a young lord and a woman. Very beautiful, very cruel.'

Telamon and Alekto, thought Pirra. Despite the heat, she felt cold. In her mind, she saw Alekto as she'd last seen her on Thalakrea: that perfect face and those empty black eyes, studying Pirra's scar with an unsettling mix of eagerness and disgust.

'Like locusts they came,' said Itineb. 'Taking our food, our cattle. But they had the favour of the Perao, and the Lord Kerasher was with them, so we had to obey.' He paused. 'My brother had a grove of date-palms. He'd planted them, he loved them like children. The Crow woman had them cut down because she wished to taste the delicacy that is the heart of a date-palm. My brother wept, and this pleased the Crow woman. She enjoyed his pain. Later that night, some of our dogs barked, and because she asked, the Lord Kerasher had them killed. She enjoyed that too.' He glanced at Hylas with dislike. 'Maybe you are Crow, maybe not. Whoever you are, you bring danger. Tomorrow you go!'

'But we need to travel to the other end of Egypt,' Pirra said hotly. 'Look at Hylas – he can't even walk! We need your help!'

Itineb rose to his feet. 'You've had all the help I will give. *If*, as you said when you got here, you have the favour of our gods – let *them* help!'

13

Pirra set a basin of water in the shade of an acacia tree and Echo swept down for her morning bathe.

Below them, women were washing clothes in the shallows, and on the bank, children were making dung-cakes for the fires. Itineb's little daughter Kawi sat apart, scowling at a mess of river clay.

Echo flapped her wings and dipped in her head, splashing and gurgling with delight. She hopped out, shook herself from beak to tail, and threw Pirra a grateful glance: *Much better!* Then she hopped back in and started all over again.

Pirra rested her chin on her knees and yawned. She'd slept on the flat roof of Itineb's house with his family, each of them shrouded like a corpse against the midges. At least, they had slept, while she lay awake, worrying.

Even with Kem's help, Hylas was far too weak to set off tomorrow. And they'd be going on foot: the villagers knew their boat was stolen, and wouldn't let them take it.

And now to learn that the Crows had tracked Userref to Pa-Sobek . . . Had they already found him?

Echo splashed Pirra in the face. Distractedly, she splashed back. The falcon slitted her eyes and gurgled. *Go on, do it again.*

I have to make them help us, thought Pirra. I have to. We can't do this on our own.

Kawi had crept up and was watching from behind the tree. She was skeletally thin: Pirra could see the skull beneath the skin, and every one of her ribs.

She asked the child in Egyptian if she wanted to splash Echo, but Kawi shook her head. She was gazing wistfully at the falcon, and picking the scabs where her eyebrows had been.

Those eyebrows . . . 'Are you grieving?' Pirra said gently. 'Is that why you shaved everything off?'

Kawi blinked. 'Our dog died,' she mumbled.

'I'm sorry. What was his name?'

'Hebny. She had the *blackest* fur.' *Hebny*. Ebony.

'I always wanted a dog,' said Pirra. 'My mother wouldn't let me.'

Kawi came a little closer. In one fist she clutched a lump of river clay, and in the other a wooden mouse with a lower jaw that you moved by a string. It reminded Pirra of the wooden leopard Userref had made when she was little.

She asked when Hebny had died, and Kawi said many days ago, the barbarians shot her because she barked.

Alekto, thought Pirra with hatred. 'Is that why you won't eat? Because they killed her?'

Kawi shook her head.

Pirra studied her strange, bony little face. 'Where's Hebny buried?' she asked.

'She's not. She isn't ready.'

Userref always said that for an Egyptian, it was vital that when you died, your loved ones made sure that your body didn't rot, so that it could be a home for your spirit. His greatest fear was that he would die outside Egypt; then he wouldn't receive the proper rites and his spirit could never be reunited with his family.

Carefully, Pirra asked the child what had to be done to get Hebny ready for burial. To her surprise, Kawi brightened up a lot. 'Oh, it takes *ages*! First we pulled out her guts and dried them and Father scraped out her brains, but we left in her heart, so the gods can weigh it, and we stuffed her full of *hesmen* and straw to get her nice and dry.'

Pirra felt slightly sick, but Kawi clearly found it a comfort. 'I made her a collar of lotus flowers and Father tied a little scroll to it with a spell so that she'll know what to say when the gods ask her questions –'

If Hebny can read, Pirra thought doubtfully.

'– and we used my big sister's old dress to wrap her up. Would you like to see?'

'Um –'

Grabbing her hand, Kawi dragged her into Itineb's house, where an oblong basket stood behind the small clay shrine to the ancestors. In the basket lay a dog-shaped bundle, bound very tight and blotched with yellow stains.

Being tied up for ever was Pirra's worst nightmare. She thought of Hebny's spirit struggling inside, and black spots swam before her eyes. 'She can't move,' she mumbled.

'Course she can, this is just where her spirit comes for a rest! I've done the Opening of the Mouth – sort of, so she can breathe and bark and eat . . .' Kawi's small face puckered, as if she'd suddenly remembered what was the matter. 'But it's all gone *wrong!*' she wailed. 'I'd collected everything she'll need in her grave – her ball, her favourite mat, and Mother'd made little clay foods to last for ever. I had it all in a basket, but some horrible boys threw it in the river and now everyone's too busy and I've tried to do it myself and I *can't*' – she held up the mangled lump of clay – 'so Hebny will be hungry for ever!'

The following day, Kawi had devoured an entire loaf of date bread, a pot of bean stew and a jar of barley beer, and was happily showing her astonished parents what Pirra had made: a miniature flock of river-clay sheep, a herd of tiny brindled cattle, and enough ducks, geese and pigs to keep Hebny fed for eternity.

'There are even little bones,' Kawi said proudly. 'And *look* at her new ball!'

Pirra glanced at Hylas, who gave her a wan smile. He was still frighteningly weak, but Kawi reminded him of Issi, so he'd woven a ball out of palm leaves – making sure that Havoc didn't see, or she'd have been jealous.

'Why didn't you *tell* us this was what was troubling you?' Itineb asked his daughter in Egyptian.

Kawi squirmed and mumbled something inaudible.

In bemusement, Itineb picked up a tiny brindled bullock. 'Where did you learn to do this?' he asked Pirra.

'Userref showed me.'

He put the bullock back in the basket.

'Not there,' muttered Kawi, '*here*, with the rest of the herd.'

While she was busy setting Hebny's livestock in order, Pirra turned to Itineb. 'You were wrong about us.'

'We're not Crows,' said Hylas.

Itineb rubbed the back of his neck with his stump. 'Yesterday, you asked how it comes that I speak Akean.' He paused. 'When I was a boy, my father wanted me to be a healer, so he sent me upriver to live with his cousin, who is a mat-maker outside the Temple of Pa-Sobek. It has a great market: much people from many lands. There I learnt healing, and Akean. From a scribe I even learnt a few of the *medu netjer*: the sacred signs. That scribe taught many boys from all along the River. His name is Nebetku.'

Pirra went still.

'I had heard that my teacher had a brother who was lost long ago, maybe taken by slavers or a crocodile, they never found out. So when the Crow barbarians came, and spoke that name – Userref – I remembered; though I didn't tell them.'

Again he rubbed his neck, setting his wig askew. 'Soon it will be the *heb* of the First Drop. For this, people travel to temples and make offerings.' He glanced at Kawi, busy with her basket. 'This year, I have much to give thanks for. I will journey all the way to the Temple of Pa-Sobek and give thanks for my daughter's life.' His dark eyes flicked from Pirra to Hylas. 'I will take you if you wish.'

Hylas drifted awake with no idea where he was. Heat, darkness, a swampy smell of reeds.

He was on Itineb's boat, hidden under the awning. Pirra slept with her back to him, her shoulder blades as sharp and delicate as little wings.

Yesterday they'd headed up what Itineb called 'one of the River's children'. He didn't say when they would reach the River itself. Hylas had lain in a blur of exhaustion, while Itineb and his two brothers handled the sail, and Pirra bickered with Kem, and Havoc padded restlessly up and down.

They'd had a job coaxing her on board, and in the end Hylas had lured her with the mummified Hebny, which she clearly regarded as a new plaything – although Hylas promised an anxious Kawi that he would *never* let the lioness touch her beloved pet. (It had been a relief when Itineb buried Hebny and her grave-goods in a patch of desert while Havoc was safely asleep.)

They also had a battle persuading Itineb to take Kem with them, and when they finally succeeded, Kem was so grateful he bowed low. 'Now I in your debt,' he said solemnly.

In the distance, a jackal barked.

Hylas thought back to the night of the scorpion. He dimly remembered raving in his fever to Pirra about the jackal-headed god, but he hadn't told her that he'd seen it bending over her *wedjat*. Now the memory filled him with foreboding. Had the god been warning about the scorpion? Or something else?

The sky was turning grey when he crawled out from under the awning, and the north wind cooled his skin. He felt shaky, but at least he could stand.

The Great Green had been left behind. As the banks glided past, he saw shadowy fields of flax, and mud-brick houses where families lay on flat roofs to escape the heat – and beyond, the deathlike silence of the desert.

He remembered another night-time river journey two summers before, after the Crows had attacked his camp. At the time, he'd thought that in a few days he would find Issi. Now here he was, at the edge of the world.

Kem slept on a coil of rope. Beyond him, Itineb's brothers were snoring. Echo perched in the mast with her head under her wing. The sail bellied in the wind. It was made of papyrus. The whole boat was papyrus: hull, awning, rigging. Only the oars and mast were wood. Trees were precious in this land of reeds.

Havoc picked her way towards him, stepping casually over the sleepers. She seemed to have grown used to the heat, but she was plagued by midges and she *hated* the boat; she'd been sick a lot. At times, she splashed ashore and disappeared, but always returned before they set off. Now she rubbed her head against Hylas' thigh, and he scratched her ears and felt a bit better.

Itineb sat in the stern with his stump on the steering-paddle. 'The daughter of the Sun brings us luck,' he said with a bow for Havoc. 'If this wind keeps up, we won't have to use the oars.'

'How long till Pa-Sobek?' said Hylas.

Itineb lifted his shoulders. 'With a strong wind all the way, not too many days. Without a wind – much longer.'

Either way, thought Hylas, we'll be stuck under that

mat for days. He wasn't going to be the one to tell Pirra.

'You feel stronger?' said Itineb.

'Mm. But my eyes feel scratchy and I keep sniffing.'

Itineb smiled. 'It's the end of *Shemu*, the Dry Time. We call it the time of blocked noses. But it's a good time to go upriver. The current is weak, the wind is strong, and people are too busy with the harvest to notice strangers.'

Staying hidden had been easier than Hylas had feared. Itineb's wife had given him a kilt and a long strip of linen to wind about his head and hide his fair hair, and she'd cut Pirra's hair in a fringe. Nobody had bothered disguising Kem, as no one noticed slaves. And if anyone asked about Havoc, Itineb said she was a gift for the Temple at Pa-Sobek.

Far away, a lion roared.

Havoc pricked her ears and uttered a groany *yowmp-yowmp*. She *wanted* to roar back, but she didn't know how.

'Those are the temple lions of Nay-Ta-Hut,' said Itineb.

'They keep *lions* in a temple? For sacrifice?'

'Oh, no! The priests sing to them and feed them the choicest meats, they deck them with jewels. When they die they are embalmed and buried in a special tomb. In other temples we have baboons, falcons . . . upriver there is a great lake where they keep crocodiles, to honour Sobek.'

'Who's Sobek?'

Itineb cast an uneasy glance over the side. '*Sobek* means crocodile. The Raging One: He Who Makes Women into Widows. But He also keeps the banks green, and sends the Flood.'

'So where we're going – Pa-Sobek – that means –'

'The place of the crocodile, yes.'

Hylas was dismayed. He'd hoped crocodiles had been left behind with the Great Green.

'Here. Eat.' Itineb indicated a cone-shaped loaf and a jar of soapy red beer.

Hylas had been doing his best to get used to Egyptian food. He liked the sweet chewy dates, but not the green things they called 'cucumbers'. Even familiar foods were strange. Pirra had sworn never again to eat chickpeas after learning that Egyptians called them *heru bik*: falcon's eyes. And she'd been surprised to find goat's-milk cheese, as Userref regarded goats as unclean. When she'd told Itineb, he'd laughed. 'Then your Userref is better off than me! Goats aren't unclean if you're poor!'

Just then, the boat swept round a bend and Itineb

cried out: 'We have reached Iteru-aa!' His brothers woke up and started casting offerings of barley overboard, then all three knelt in prayer.

The Sun had risen, and in the dancing air, the Great River was a deep shimmering blue, alive with waterbirds and brilliant white egrets. Along its banks were rippling green papyrus and spiky date-palms, and beyond lay fields of golden stubble, huddled villages and lion-coloured hills.

'Iteru-aa,' repeated Itineb, his eyes brimming with tears. 'See how beautiful!'

Hylas did not reply. It *was* beautiful, but as never before, he felt the *strangeness* of Egypt: strange creatures, strange gods – and now this vast, mysterious river. He didn't belong here. How would he ever get home?

Pirra had woken up, and from her face, he could tell that she felt it too. She pointed to the hills on the west bank. 'Are those tombs?'

Itineb nodded. 'The Houses of Eternity. The East Bank is for the living, the West Bank is for the Dead.'

'But it has fields and villages,' said Hylas.

'Of course! Tomb-diggers, coffin-makers, linen-weavers – they all have to live.' Itineb took a deep breath of the swampy air, and smiled. 'It begins and ends with the River. When we are born, we take our first bath in it. It gives us mud for our houses, fish to eat, linen to wear, papyrus for boats. It gives us an easy road for moving about: north with the current, south with the wind; and it is easy to cross from one bank to the other, if you know the currents and the sandbanks. Finally when we die, we take our last bath in it, and rest in a tomb plastered with its mud.' He glanced at Hylas. 'Have you no river in your country?'

'A few. Nothing like this.'

'They say you have whole hills covered in trees.'

'Yes, we call them forests.'

Itineb raised his eyebrows, as if suspecting a joke. 'What trees? Date-palms?'

'No. Pines, oaks, firs, but no date-palms.'

'No date-palms?' Itineb shook his head in pity. 'My brother would hate that.'

'But in summer we have lots of flowers.' Hylas felt a stab of homesickness. 'And rain – that's water falling from the sky – and in winter when it's cold, it goes white and fluffy, we call it snow.'

Itineb laughed. 'Ah, now I know you're making it up!'

Pirra woke to a glare of sunlight and the hum of many voices. For one terrifying moment, she thought she was back on Keftiu. Then she saw Hylas peering from under the awning. His back was rigid with tension.

'Hylas get out of sight . . .' Itineb's voice receded as he ran to the steering-paddle. 'We're passing Ineb-Hedj!'

For a moment, Pirra saw only the crows wheeling overhead. She thought of Telamon and Alekto, and shuddered. Then she saw the town on the East Bank and her spirit quailed. It was even more immense than the House of the Goddess. In awe she took in towering stone walls and columns carved like lotus flowers. Swarms of people: men piling ox-carts with watermelons, bundles of sesame and linen; women holding flapping bundles of waterfowl by their feet.

And so many boats! At a quayside, men loaded a great wooden cargo ship with giant blocks of stone. Beside it, on a richly painted vessel with a curving prow, a yellow canopy fluttered in the wind. And everywhere smaller craft – boats, punts, canoes – all heading up, down and across the River with casual skill.

Hylas touched her arm and pointed west. 'Why would men build such things?' he said hoarsely.

In the distance, Pirra made out three astonishing mountains rising from the desert. Their triangular sides were impossibly straight and their smooth flanks blazed with colour: red, yellow, green, blue. Their searing gold peaks pierced the sky.

'They call them *Mer*,' muttered Kem. 'Places of Ascension. Perao's ancestors built them long ago to climb the sky and be gods.'

Pirra stared at the enormous stone tombs and felt the power of Egypt tightening like a fist around her heart. That power was on the side of the Crows. Against it, what chance had she and Hylas?

Back beneath the awning, she took out her amulet. The Eye of Heru was made of heavy bronze. The upper eyelid was red jasper, the iris and brow were deep blue lapis – and so was the mark of the falcon, the thick line that swept down from the lower lid, like a tear.

Years before, Userref's older brother had lent it to him when they were boys and the family had gone on pilgrimage to Ineb-Hedj. 'You can keep it for today but *don't* lose it,' Nebetku had warned. But that was the day when Userref had strayed and been taken by slavers. He'd felt guilty about the *wedjat* for years.

Pirra lay clutching the amulet, listening to the harsh cries of crows. She thought of Telamon and Alekto gliding upriver in their black ship. She felt afraid.

Days and nights slid by, and still the wind blew, speeding them south. They glided past Waset, the beating heart of Egypt, that was even greater than Ineb-Hedj; and past countless temples: Abedju, Dobd, Nekhen: City of the Falcon . . .

At last, the River narrowed and grew choppy. Itineb and his brothers had to take care steering past rocks and sandbanks where crocodiles basked. There were fewer villages. On either side, cliffs loomed.

Kem looked about him eagerly. 'Not far to my country. Soon I leave and head across the desert.'

Hylas felt a pang. He'd grown to like Kem. 'What will you do when you get there?'

'Find my village and my family. Then prove I am brave.'

Hylas remembered the rite of manhood: stealing a weapon from an Egyptian warrior. 'We could do that now, on the way,' he said. 'We could creep ashore. I'm a pretty good thief.'

Kem looked surprised. Then he laughed and clapped Hylas on the shoulder. 'You a good friend – but it wouldn't work. I got to do it by my own self, when men of my tribe are watching – so they know I don't lie!'

That sounded unnecessarily harsh to Hylas, but from what Kem had told him of Wawat, it was a harsh land.

Around midnight, the boat jolted to a halt. Hylas emerged to see Havoc leap into the shallows and vanish in a swamp. Above him, stony hills blotted out the stars.

Kem's dark face was alight with excitement. 'Pa-Sobek just round that bend! From there it not far to my country!'

Together, they jumped ashore. Itineb was speaking urgently with two men standing by an ox-cart. Pirra was trying to follow what they said.

'These are friends of my cousin,' Itineb told Hylas in Akean. 'Tomb-builders from the village of Tjebu on the West Bank. You can trust them.'

'Oh yes?' Hylas said suspiciously.

'They say Nebetku is in hiding from the Crows.'

'*They say,*' repeated Hylas.

'I've told them you are friends,' said Itineb. 'They will take you to him – but you must go blindfold.'

'No,' Hylas said flatly.

'It's a trap,' muttered Kem.

Pirra chewed her lip. 'But we trust Itineb, don't we? If he says they're all right, I think we should believe him.'

Kem was shaking his head. 'Don't do it, Hylas.'

Hylas looked from Itineb to the men. They were burly, their faces lined by hardship; no clues there. He nodded slowly. 'I agree with Pirra. We'll have to take the risk.'

Kem backed away. 'Then we must part sooner than I like.' Putting his fist to his breast, he bowed to Hylas, then Pirra. 'I thank you, my friends. You made them bring me on the boat. Without you I could not reach here. I owe you much.'

'No, you don't,' said Hylas. 'You saved us in the desert.'

'Cho!' Kem brushed that aside. Then he grinned at Pirra. 'Some day I make you to know I'm no coward!'

'Kem, I *know* you're not.'

'But some day I prove it! Good luck, my friends. May your gods go with you. Say goodbye to Havoc for me!' With that he disappeared into the night, leaving Hylas reflecting bitterly that once again, he'd lost a friend.

After that, things happened fast. Itineb and his brothers swiftly took their leave and headed upriver, while the two men – Hylas never learnt their names – motioned him and Pirra into the cart. They were allowed to keep their weapons, but blindfolded, their hands bound.

The cart jolted along for some time, then they were helped into a boat: Hylas guessed they were crossing to the West Bank. He asked Pirra if she was all right. She said a tense, 'Mm.' He whistled to Havoc and heard her distant call.

Now they were out of the boat and in another cart, then they were led over rough ground and through a doorway. Hylas smelt wood shavings and wet clay. He heard a man's painful wrenching cough. His hands were untied, the blindfold pulled off.

He was in some kind of workshop, with Pirra beside him. By the glimmer of tallow lamps, he made out a palm-log roof and a floor of trodden earth. Around the walls were rows of shadowy clay people about a hand high.

Before him stood two men, both Egyptians. One was skeletally thin, with straggling grey hair that contrasted oddly with his youngish face. The other was twice Hylas' age but only half his height, with the stumpy legs and bulging head of a dwarf. Both were armed with curved knives and flinty expressions. They were guarding a third man who sat cross-legged on a mat. Pirra was staring at him fixedly.

He had once been handsome, and his features were vaguely familiar, but his eyes were sunken, his face wasted by sickness. It was also smeared with lime, heightening his likeness to a skull, and he'd shaved off his hair and even his eyebrows.

Hylas' belly tightened. Egyptians did that when they were in mourning.

Pirra said something shaky in Egyptian.

The sick man glared at her and spat a retort.

'What does he say?' said Hylas.

She'd gone white to the lips. 'He asks why we come to – to trouble his grief.'

Oh, no, thought Hylas.

'Yes – grief,' croaked the man in heavily accented Akean. 'I am Nebetku. My brother Userref is *dead*. You barbarians killed him! My brother is *dead*!'

15

'It's not true,' said Pirra. But every thud of her heart drove it deeper. Dead, dead, dead.

'Thirteen days we had together . . .' gasped the sick man. 'So many years apart. He knew they were after him – their filthy barbarian dagger . . .'

'He can't be dead,' Pirra said numbly. 'Not Userref.'

'Who *are* you?' Nebetku's fever-bright gaze pierced hers. 'Itined said you knew my brother – but you're barbarian – and yet you speak Egyptian. How?'

'Userref t-taught me. He –'

'What's he saying?' broke in Hylas.

'I never knew a time without him,' Pirra went on shakily. 'He was my slave, but he called me his little sister –'

'*You!* You were the one who made him swear to guard that cursed thing with his life!'

She swayed. 'Yes. I made him swear.'

'You killed him!' screamed Nebetku. 'It's because of *you* that he's dead!'

Nebetku raged on between bouts of rib-cracking coughs, and Pirra stood there and took it. Hylas couldn't understand what was said, but he could see that every word was a blow to her heart.

'He says I killed him,' she whispered, scarcely moving her lips. 'And he's right.'

'No, he's not,' Hylas said angrily. 'The Crows killed him, not you!' He turned to Nebetku. 'Tell us how he died – and speak Akean, so I can understand!'

He spoke harshly, and the dwarf and the grey-haired man glared at him and fingered their knives.

Hylas drew his own. 'What is this place?' he cried. 'Who are these people?'

To his surprise, Nebetku bared his teeth in a skeletal grin. 'Haven't you guessed? Look around you, barbarian!'

In the flickering lamplight, the rows of little clay people watched Hylas with blank painted eyes. Through the doorway, he saw more workshops. Heaped outside were bales of linen and piles of salt, long baskets and wooden boxes that looked like coffins. In the distance, he saw the glimmer of village cooking-fires, and shadowy fields rising to cliffs pocked with many caves.

'The Houses of Eternity,' croaked Nebetku. 'Everyone here works for the Dead.' He coughed into his hands, then held them up. They were smeared with blood. 'Soon I will become one of them.'

Hylas sheathed his knife. 'Tell us what happened to Userref.'

The sick man shut his eyes and fought for breath. Gently, the dwarf touched his shoulder – but he frowned, determined to speak. 'He feared for his life . . . And he mourned his "little sister". He thought she was dead.'

Pirra bowed her head.

'He knew the Crow barbarians were seeking him,' Nebetku went on, 'but he grew tired of hiding . . . Without telling us, he crossed to Pa-Sobek, to make an offering. He was in disguise, but the barbarians caught him – or the spies of Kerasher, whom the Perao had sent to help them, we don't know which.' His gaunt face worked. 'They beat him savagely. "Where is our dagger?" But my brother was brave, he never told.'

Pirra pressed both hands to her mouth.

'Somehow, he broke free – still with his arms tied behind. He must have known he had only moments before they caught him so he ran to the jetty . . . He leapt in the River – he gave himself to Iteru . . . And Iteru carried him away and he drowned.'

Hylas heard the sputtering lamps and the rasp of the sick man's breath. Pirra stood with her fists clenched at her sides. Her face was stony, her scar livid on her cheek. 'Did you find the body?' she said quietly.

'What do you care?' spat Nebetku.

'I loved him too!' she flashed out. 'I know how much it mattered to him to be properly buried!'

Nebetku didn't respond. 'Soon I also will die,' he said wearily. 'No more coughing, no more pain. Death will be my recovery, and I will be with my brother for eternity . . .'

'Where's the dagger?' insisted Hylas.

Nebetku opened his eyes. 'That's all you barbarians think about.'

'I'm sorry but I need to know.'

But Nebetku broke into a terrible fit of coughing, and his friends closed protectively around him, shooing Hylas away and jabbering at him in Egyptian. With a jolt, he saw that Pirra was gone, stumbling out into the night as if she didn't care where she went.

Pirra sat on the bank, watching the black River sliding past. He can't be dead. How can that be? How can it be that I'll never see him again?

Dimly, she took in reeds and date-palms around her. Sandbanks ahead. Choppy water surrounding a small dark island spiked with trees. And over on the East Bank, the flickering fires of a large town. That must be Pa-Sobek. Where he drowned. She couldn't take it in.

A large chilly nose nudged her elbow. It was Havoc. The young lioness was wet from swimming the River, and she leant against Pirra, trying to comfort with her nearness. Pirra couldn't bring herself to stroke her. She felt hollow. Nothing inside but disbelief.

Echo lit on to her shoulder. Dimly, Pirra was aware of cool talons pricking her skin, and the moth's-wing touch of feathers. Usually, the falcon tugged her hair and asked for meat. Tonight she simply perched. Pirra was grateful for that.

Hylas came and touched her arm. She told him to go away.

'Pirra,' he said gently. 'You're too close to the River. There might be crocodiles.'

It was pointless to argue, so she let him lead her somewhere else. Echo flew off, and Havoc seemed to decide there were too many strangers about, and vanished into the night.

They stopped at another workshop, this one dark and empty, with coffins stacked outside. They sat with their backs against one. Pirra felt the warmth of Hylas' shoulder and thigh against hers. She thought: he is alive and Userref is dead. It isn't possible . . .

An appalling idea came to her. 'What happened to his body? It wasn't – he wasn't eaten by crocodiles?'

'No, the River protected him. Someone found him washed up among reeds.' He paused. 'I didn't make that up – I asked Nebetku just now.'

She nodded.

'Pirra, this isn't your fault.'

'Yes it is.'

'No. The Crows killed Userref. Not you.'

The dwarf appeared. He was half Pirra's size, but he carried himself with an authority that demanded respect. 'I am Rensi,' he told her brusquely. 'I am *shabti*-maker and friend of Nebetku. I am taking you back across the River.'

Pirra translated for Hylas, who crossed his arms on his chest. 'Tell him we're not going without the dagger.'

Rensi snorted. Three burly stonemasons appeared, along with the grey-haired man. 'This is Herihor,' the dwarf told Pirra. 'The others you do not need to know their names. Come. You will do as I say.'

As she sat in the prow of the boat, Pirra was dimly aware that Hylas was still arguing in Akean, and Rensi and Herihor were berating him in Egyptian. It was all meaningless. Why couldn't Hylas forget about the dagger?

Vaguely, she noticed that they weren't heading straight across the River, but in a wide, indirect arc. Hylas had noticed, too. 'Ask them why,' he said suspiciously. She did, and was told that the current was bad on the shorter route, with dangerous rocks beneath the surface. She wished Hylas would leave her in peace.

She smelt the swampy River and watched Echo wheeling across the stars. '*When you die,*' Userref had said once, '*if you are buried with the proper rites, your spirit will grow the wings of a falcon. Then you can fly out and be with the gods under the Sun, only returning to your tomb at night, for a rest . . .*'

Tears stung her eyes. Fiercely, she blinked them back. At least he died in Egypt, she told herself. He always wanted that.

Out loud, she asked Rensi if Userref had been given a good burial, with the proper rites.

Her question seemed to outrage the dwarf. He glared at her, then turned his back and ignored her for the rest of the crossing.

At the East Bank, they moored in a deserted inlet fringed with acacia trees. In the moonlight, Pirra glimpsed fields of stubble beyond, and shadowy rows of beanstalks.

'Where are we?' Hylas said suspiciously.

'Sh!' hissed Herihor. Then to Pirra, 'It's not good to speak loudly even here, there may be spies. You must go back now, back to your own land.'

'*What*? But we don't even know where we are!'

Herihor shooed her away with his long bony hands. 'That is not our concern! Go now, back to your own lands!'

With the others, he headed for the boat – but suddenly Rensi turned and waddled back to Hylas and Pirra. He was still seething with anger, incensed by Pirra's question about burial rites. 'You,' he jabbed his finger at Hylas, 'shut up.' To Pirra: 'You should be *ashamed*! Of *course* we buried him well! Do you think we would neglect one of our own? The brother of Nebetku?'

'What's he saying?' said Hylas. 'Ask him about the dagger!'

'I am *shabti*-maker,' fumed Rensi, his voice shaking with rage. 'You know what is *shabti*? Little people who work for you in the Duat, when you are dead! For him I made the *finest shabti*! And Herihor there . . .' he pointed at the grey-haired man, 'he is embalmer. Other friends are garland-maker, mixer of unguents. Nebetku himself is great scribe! We gave Userref – may his name be spoken always in the mouths of the living – a burial fit for Perao himself!'

He gulped for breath. 'You will ask how we managed this so quickly and I will tell you! Last year, Nebetku got everything ready for his own death – so now for his brother, we had it all! Coffin, amulets, Spells for Coming Forth by Day – all we had to do was change the names! As for the body, well, Herihor is best embalmer I've ever seen, he *lives* for his Wrapped Ones, he prefers them to the living! He took out the insides, all nice and clean . . .'

Pirra put her hands to her mouth.

'. . . he purified the body with *hesmen* and resin, even *myrrh*, which Nebetku had been saving for himself. When Herihor finished with that Wrapped One, you'd think it was *alive*! Skin plumped up, *wadju* on the eyes, beautiful wig of real hair! And that coffin!' He kissed his fingertips. 'No cheap basketwork, oh no, *sycomore wood*, painted inside and out! And then for the burial – we paid wailers, we sang prayers, we filled the tomb with food, the proper garlands – everything perfect, everything *right*!'

'Pirra,' Hylas broke in impatiently.

Rensi shot him a withering look. 'This barbarian cares only for his dagger! But didn't I tell you that we followed Userref's *every wish*? He'd told Nebetku that if he died, the cursed thing must be wrapped in spells begging the gods to destroy it – so this we did! He wanted it buried with him – this also we did!'

Pirra blinked. 'What? You buried the dagger with him?'

Rensi flung up his stumpy arms. 'Did I not say so? Are you barbarians deaf as well as stupid?'

Numbly, Pirra told Hylas in Akean.

His jaw dropped. 'It's in his *tomb*?'

She nodded.

He thought for a moment. 'Right. Well then we've got to get it out.'

She stared at him. 'We can't break into his tomb!'

'We've got to.'

'No, Hylas. Listen. Rensi says it was buried with a spell asking the gods to destroy it. Surely we can leave them to –'

'No, we can't! To the gods, ten thousand years are like the blink of an eye, they might not do it in our lifetime!'

'But –'

'Besides, if the Crows could find Userref, they can find his tomb. We've got to get there first!'

He was right, but just for an instant, Pirra hated him for it.

'Tell the dwarf,' he urged her. 'Tell him we have to get the dagger out now.'

Predictably, Rensi exploded. 'Break into his *tomb*? You barbarians are all the same! Well thanks be to Ausar, Greatest of the Great, his tomb is beyond your reach!'

'What do you mean?' said Pirra.

The dwarf stomped up and down – then put his hands on his hips and glared up at her. 'Nebetku's family tomb,' he said in a furious whisper, 'was dug by his ancestors long ago, when they were out of favour with the Hati-aa. They dug it in a secret place, so it could never be harmed: they hid it as only those who know every stone in the Houses of Eternity can hide. Years passed, they came back into favour – but *always* they kept their tomb hidden! Now only Nebetku and a few trusted friends,' he pounded his barrel chest, 'know where it is – and we will *never* tell! No one will *ever* find this tomb! Not if you searched for more years than there are sands in the desert could you find it!'

16

'Time is running out,' Telamon told Meritamen, the Hati-aa's young wife, 'and you still haven't found my dagger.'

'I will soon,' she said quietly.

'What does that mean?'

A slave staggered between them with a giant bunch of blue cornflowers and scarlet poppies, followed by three maidservants bearing baskets piled with loaves. At least, Telamon *thought* they were loaves. Each was shaped like a cow, with brindled markings of mashed dates, and large roast-almond eyes.

These people decorate everything, he thought in disgust. Even bread. Out loud, he said to Meritamen: 'Tell me what's going on and stop hiding behind all this.'

She flinched at his tone. Behind her, her little sister clutched her cat in her arms. 'I'm not hiding,' she replied coolly. 'But tomorrow is the start of the *heb*, and the Hati-aa's household must do its part. I have much to see to . . .' A wave of her hand took in the courtyard bustling with barbers and linen-pleaters, garland-weavers and music-makers.

All the useless people, Telamon thought scornfully. Why would anyone keep slaves just to make *music*?

To his astonishment, Meritamen turned her back on him to give orders. How *dare* she, a girl, ignore a warrior of the House of Koronos?

Rage churned within him. To be thwarted by *women* . . . He was only here now because Alekto had said he might get more out of Meritamen than she. 'I've done what I can with the girl,' she'd yawned. 'It's your turn, nephew.' That was typical of Alekto, presuming to give him orders! And now this girl Meritamen was calmly walking away . . .

'I haven't finished,' he barked. With a jerk of his head, he told her to follow: A deliberate insult that made her flush.

'Listen to me,' he said when they'd reached a quiet corner of the garden. 'I can break you if I want. Look at me when I'm talking to you!'

Reluctantly, she obeyed. Her dark eyes were rimmed

with black, the upper lids painted brilliant green; like the stone goddesses outside the Temple, he thought with a twinge of unease.

'I have been patient,' he went on in a low voice. 'At your request, I've even moored my ship behind that island in the River, so that the sight of it won't offend your gods. I've done all this because you promised to find my dagger.'

'And I will,' she said.

'I gave you until the Day of the First Drop,' he continued. 'That's two days away. If by then I don't hold the dagger in my fist, the Perao will know that it's your fault. I will see you and your husband stripped of power, your names obliterated, your family ruined. Do you doubt that I can do this?'

'No,' she said with a look of cold dislike. 'Now please, I must prepare to take my place in the *heb* –'

'I don't *care* about your wretched procession!'

'Well you should!' Darting a glance over her shoulder, she leant closer, and he caught her scent of jasmine and cinnamon. 'I don't know where your dagger is hidden,' she breathed, 'but I will soon, and to find out, I must be at the *heb*!'

'*Why?*'

'I can't tell you! Just believe that I know how to make them give it to me –'

'Who's "them"?'

'Let me do this my way!'

Was this a trick? Was she laughing at him behind that pretty, painted face?

'All right,' he said. 'But I'll go with you to the *heb* –'

'*No!*'

'Oh, yes. I'm watching you. And if you're deceiving me . . .' He shot a threatening glance at the little sister, who was peering from behind a pomegranate tree. 'And don't imagine,' he told Meritamen, 'that you can hide your sister somewhere safe. The Lady Alekto has asked Kerasher to set his slaves to watch her. From now on, your sister will never be out of their sight.'

Meritamen's eyes widened with alarm. 'That is not necessary,' she faltered.

So he was right. This was how to control her: through the sister. 'The Lady Alekto thinks it is,' he replied, 'and so do I. No more argument. I'm coming with you to the *heb*.' He was beginning to enjoy himself. And it occurred to him that he would go to the *heb* without telling Alekto. He felt a flicker of fear at the idea, which he swiftly suppressed. It was time to show Alekto who was in command.

'Then come if you wish,' said Meritamen. 'But stay away from me, or you'll ruin everything.'

'So you do know how to get it back.'

'Oh yes,' she retorted with startling bitterness. 'I know a way, though it is cruel beyond anything even you barbarians could do, and I am *ashamed* to do it! But to save my family, I will make myself cruel. I will find your dagger – because I must. And then you and your kind will leave Pa-Sobek and never trouble us again!'

The lion cub was desperate to leave this horrible land and never come back.

She'd had enough of flies, river pigs and giant lizards. For the boy's sake, she'd braved the strange humans – even the one who was missing his forepaw and whose mane came *right off* when he scratched his head. She'd endured many Lights and Darks on that wobbly bundle of reeds which gave her a nasty feeling, as if she was going to sick up a furball, but never did. And when the boy and the girl had got into *another* bundle of reeds and crossed the Great Wet, she'd seized her courage by the scruff and swum after them.

But now, just as she'd shaken the wet from her pelt, they'd crossed the Great Wet *again*. She dared not swim after them this time, not even for the boy. There were too many humans over there. She was simply too scared.

Why was everything so chewed up? It was harder

and harder to keep the pride together. As soon as she'd got used to the dark boy, he'd left, and now some terrible sadness was gnawing the girl, biting so deep that not even a muzzle-rub could help. What made things even worse was that the falcon was so distracted by all the ducks that it didn't seem to bother her that the pride was falling apart.

Mewing in distress, the lion cub prowled the bank. The boy hadn't called for her, and she sensed that he wanted her to stay on this side, which made her feel even more left out.

What was he *doing* over there? Couldn't he smell that there were far too many humans? Why couldn't he stay here, among the lairs of the dead ones, and the ghosts, who were no bother to anyone?

The falcon alighted on her back and companionably pecked off some ticks. The lion cub envied the falcon. She never got scared. Why would she, when she could fly away whenever she wanted?

Besides, the falcon actually *liked* this awful place.

The falcon much preferred this side of the Great Wet. There were only a couple of falcons on the cliffs, and they were keeping their distance – and not too many humans.

The falcon liked the sick one best, as he reminded

her of the first human she'd ever seen, who'd rescued her from ants when she was a fledgling and fell out of the Nest. The sick human coughed, but spoke to her respectfully, and he'd put a dead lark for her on a boulder. She'd gulped a few beakfuls and tucked the rest in a hole for later. She couldn't eat when she was worried about the girl.

Human feelings were twisty and hard to follow, like the bumpy air before a storm; but the falcon could tell that the girl was sad. The falcon had tried to make her feel better, but she didn't think it had worked.

The Sun was coming up, and the falcon spotted ducks nibbling among the reeds, and was instantly distracted. Her feathers tingled. She longed to hunt.

This place was *made* for falcons. Why didn't the others like it? The lion cub hated it, and as for the boy and the girl, at first, the falcon had thought they liked it as much as she did, because they'd made themselves *look* like falcons, by smearing black stripes under their eyes. But now she sensed that they disliked it as much as the lion cub. This made everything so complicated that the falcon was nearly tempted to fly off and never come back.

And now the boy and girl had gone across the Great Wet *again*, to where all those humans were flocking together. *Why?*

The lion cub padded over to the falcon and flicked her a glance. *What do we do now?*

The falcon half spread her wings to cool them, then stretched out one foot and tidied her leg feathers. She was too proud to admit it, but she didn't know.

Worse than that, she was scared. There were simply too *many* humans on the other side: a vast, smelly, jostling, noisy flock.

The last thing the falcon wanted was to go anywhere near them.

17

A man thrust a basket of figs at Hylas and jabbered in Egyptian. Hylas shook his head and mimed *I can't speak*. With a shrug the man moved off into the crowd to badger someone else.

A motherly woman cast Hylas a pitying glance. He drew the end of his head-wrapping across his face and turned away. It was hard to blend in when he was taller than most Egyptians. And the Crows might be anywhere. Where was Pirra?

The air was thick with incense, the crowd so tightly packed he could hardly breathe. Peasant girls crowned with white egret feathers chatted and waved papyrus flowers. Old women hawked beer, date cakes, fried fish wrapped in palm fronds. Hylas glimpsed several black faces; Kem had said that his people came to

Pa-Sobek to trade ivory and ostrich eggs. Everyone was jostling for a place on the tree-lined avenue that led from the Temple to the River. And along its length, huge black basalt falcons perched on granite plinths, frowning at eternity with sharp golden eyes.

Itineb had described the *heb* as a great procession, when images of the gods were loaded on to sacred barges and borne up the River, to ensure that it rose again. 'It's the most important time: if the Flood is too weak, the crops die and we starve; too strong, and whole villages are washed away.'

Hylas didn't care about that, he just wanted to find Pirra.

I have to see where Userref died, she'd said as she ran off. Was she mad enough to try to reach the jetty?

The Sun had only just risen, but it felt like ages since Rensi had left them under the acacia trees. 'We've got to get back to the West Bank,' Hylas had told her. 'That's where the tomb must be, that's where the dagger is.'

'I don't care about the dagger,' she'd said wearily. 'No one will ever find it now.'

'The Crows will, if they catch Nebetku or his friends.'

'They'll never tell.'

'They will if they're tortured.'

That had gone through her like a knife. Hylas had felt bad about hurting her, and furious with the Crows for causing such grief – but there was no *time*. 'As long as the dagger exists, the Crows can't be beaten! You don't want to live the rest of your life in fear!'

But she'd only hugged herself and rocked back and forth.

'Pirra, this isn't like you! Time to grieve later –'

'What do you know about grief?'

He'd flinched. 'Two moons ago, I learnt that my mother was dead.'

'So did I.'

'You hated your mother!'

'You never even knew yours!'

There was a shocked silence. Both knew they'd gone too far.

'This isn't helping,' Hylas had said. 'What we need is –'

He never finished. Torchlight had appeared between the trees and suddenly a throng was upon them: peasants from outlying villages, making for the *heb*.

To Hylas' horror, Pirra had run to join them. 'What are you *doing*?' he'd whispered.

'No one will notice! Hylas I have to do this, I have to see where he died!'

So here he was at the *heb*, and despite his attempts

to reach the jetty, the crowd was hustling him the other way, towards the Temple that towered over Pa-Sobek. Its massive walls throbbed with blue zigzags and red and yellow stripes. Columns shaped like giant papyrus flowers guarded its vast copper-studded gates. Itineb had said that within lay a secret world ruled by an army of priests, and tended by washerwomen, gardeners, perfume-mixers, butchers, wig-makers, weavers and those who ran the crocodile hatchery on the sacred lake.

A roar went up from the crowd as the gates were flung wide, and out came shaven-headed priests playing silver flutes and ivory clappers carved like slender hands. Behind them swayed more priests, bearing man-high pillars woven of flowers: purple nightshade, blue and white lotus, green papyrus. Then still more priests. On their shoulders they bore a litter: a platform of gilded wood. On it rested a limestone slab garlanded with willow, and on this lay a gleaming greenstone crocodile. Sobek: He Who Makes the River Rise.

The crocodile god was draped in white linen beaded with turquoise and lapis, and about His neck was a golden collar. From His warty forehead rose a plume of ostrich feathers dyed green. His thick muscular tail flopped over the end of the slab, and His claws gripped its edges – as if at any moment He might slither off it and over the heads of the crowd.

Around Hylas, people were sinking to their knees. Feeling horribly exposed, he edged backwards, bumping into a water-carrier, who scowled at him.

Hylas withdrew behind the plinth of one of the basalt falcons. Still no sign of Pirra.

After the crocodile god came more pillars of flowers in blue clouds of incense, then another gilded litter, supported by poles borne by slaves as black as Kem. Rich swathes of painted linen hung from this litter and swept the ground. Above it, a crimson canopy shaded its occupant, a fat Egyptian with a jewelled collar and an elaborate, braided wig. Tapping his chins with an ebony flywhisk, he scanned the crowd.

'Kerasher,' murmured someone in the crowd. Hylas' belly turned over. Nebetku had said that the Perao had sent Kerasher to help the Crows find the dagger. If he was here, surely they were, too.

After Kerasher's litter came another, bearing a pretty girl: his daughter? Sister? Her dark hair was twined with purple moorhen feathers, and she was surreptitiously scolding a smaller child. The child was naked but for a wreath of poppies, and clearly bored. As Hylas watched, she wriggled off the litter and into the crowd.

At that moment, Hylas spotted Pirra on the other side of the avenue. She hadn't seen him – she was looking the other way.

He couldn't risk shouting. Wildly, he waved at her from behind his plinth. But at that moment, the ground gave a sickening lurch. Lights flashed behind his eyes, and the burning finger stabbed his temples.

The din of flutes and clappers became a dull boom, and his senses turned infinitely sharp. He heard a bead of sweat trickling down the water-carrier's spine, and the crunch of beetle jaws gnawing lotuses in a garland. Then the air flooded with dreadful brightness – and on the gilded litter, Sobek turned His greenstone head and glared at him.

Hylas cried out. A shadow fell across his face. He glanced up. He saw the giant falcon twist its basalt neck to peer down at him. He fled, blundering into the water-carrier, who turned – and instead of a human face, Hylas met the fierce yellow glare of a baboon.

Blindly, he crashed through the throng.

He found himself at the mouth of a passageway between tall houses. There, crouching by a pile of rubble, was the naked child from the pretty girl's litter, crooning over a fistful of fallen feathers.

Hylas smelt her garlicky breath and heard the tiny

pinch of a snake's scales slithering out of the rubble. In a flash, he knew what was going to happen. Whipping out his knife, he threw it. The child jerked up her head. She shouted and squirmed as he snatched her to safety. In the litter nosing its way past the mouth of the passage, the pretty girl turned and saw them. Her dark eyes widened as she took in her sister wriggling in Hylas' arms – and the cobra lying skewered and thrashing on the ground.

Pirra had seen him too, and was pushing towards him.

Setting down the child, Hylas finished off the snake. As he straightened up, he saw Telamon.

The grandson of Koronos had a litter of his own, some distance behind the girl's. Hylas couldn't see his face but he knew him at once. In one frozen heartbeat, he took in his one-time friend's red linen tunic and dark warrior braids with the little clay discs at the ends. The jasper sealstone on his wrist, and the tiny amethyst falcon that had been Pirra's.

Telamon sat scanning the crowd, one forearm resting on his knee, his head turned away from Hylas. At any moment, he would see Pirra.

Frantically, Hylas waved at her to get down. 'Down!' he mouthed. 'Get down!'

She didn't understand. *What?*

Telamon's gaze was raking towards her.

Suddenly the crowd surged forwards and hid Pirra behind a forest of waving hands. They were crying out in excitement, reaching towards Echo, who'd alighted on the basalt head of the falcon god. A falcon, perched on an image of Heru! This was the best possible omen for the Flood.

Thank you, Echo, Hylas told her silently. To his relief, he saw that Pirra had realized the threat, and vanished.

But now it was Hylas who was exposed, as the crowd thinned and Telamon's gaze came sweeping towards him. Wildly, Hylas cast about for somewhere to hide.

'Here! Under here!' whispered a voice nearby. It was the pretty girl, beckoning from her litter.

Pirra appeared beside Hylas and grabbed his hand.

Just before Telamon saw them, the pretty girl twitched aside the hanging at the base of her litter – and Hylas and Pirra ducked underneath.

18

'This has to be a trap,' muttered Hylas as they shuffled blindly along under the litter.

Above him a girl's voice hissed at them in Egyptian.

'She says be quiet,' whispered Pirra, 'Telamon's close behind. – You're very pale, are you all right?'

He nodded, but it was all he could do to keep from lurching into the unseen slaves who were carrying the litter. Pirra was small enough to stand upright beneath it, but he was forced into an awkward stoop, and still reeling from his visions.

Abruptly, the litter turned and the din of the crowd fell away. Hylas parted the hangings, and came face to face with a wall. Same on the other side.

Ducking out from under, he and Pirra found

themselves in a shadowy passage between tall houses. Ten paces ahead, people stood with their backs to them, watching the procession. Behind, four sturdy black slaves blocked their escape.

In a heartbeat, their knives were taken, their arms pinioned behind their backs. But instead of a triumphant Telamon appearing at the mouth of the passage, the Egyptian girl leant out from her litter and said something to Pirra that Hylas didn't understand.

Pirra spat back defiantly.

'Sh!' The girl pointed at the procession, where Telamon's litter was nosing into view. In heavily accented Akean she said: 'I've told Kerasher I'm sick, but we haven't much time!'

They were shrouded in linen and smuggled on to a cart, then a boat – then laid none too gently on cold stone.

Wriggling out of his shroud, Hylas found himself in what appeared to be a stable, although it was far grander than any he'd ever seen. It had walls of polished limestone, painted with chariots and hunting dogs. There was a marble water trough in a corner, and sheets of wet linen hanging from the roofbeams and stirring gently in a breeze from a high window, presumably to cool the horses he could hear snorting and stamping in adjacent stalls.

Pirra lay beside him, dusty, dishevelled and furious. Like him, her arms were pinioned behind her.

Without a word, they shuffled round till they were back to back. Hylas tried to untie her, then she tried to untie him. Couldn't be done. The bindings were tight at elbows and wrists, and their fingers were numb.

Struggling to his feet, Hylas peered out of the window.

'Where are we?' said Pirra.

He couldn't see the River, as the window gave on to the cliffs. They were in shadow, the Sun dipping behind them. 'The West Bank,' he said.

To the north, in the distance, he saw fields, a large village, and many people. Nearer, what looked like the workshops where last night they'd met Nebetku. And nearer still, a trail snaked west, towards a gap in the cliffs that might be a gorge. He wondered if it led out into the desert: a possible means of escape.

Behind him, Pirra was on her feet, looking over the partition into the next-door stall. 'What are chariot horses doing out here?'

'They belong to my husband,' said the Egyptian girl, appearing in the doorway. 'The hunting is better on the West Bank. Fewer people, more prey.'

A slave held the door of their stall open while she stepped inside, nudging aside a strand of straw with one narrow sandalled foot. Behind her, two more slaves stood at a respectful distance, their arms crossed on their chests.

'Who are you?' demanded Pirra.

As if Pirra hadn't spoken, the girl nodded to the first slave. He cut their bindings, yanked off Hylas' head-covering, then withdrew with a bow. His mistress stared in fascination at Hylas' fair hair.

'Who are you?' he said, rubbing the feeling back into his wrists.

'They bound you too tight,' she replied. 'I'm sorry.'

He shrugged. 'I've had worse.'

'I can see.' Her eyes flickered over the scars on his arms and chest, and a flush stole up her cheeks.

Pirra snarled at her in Egyptian.

The girl looked her scornfully up and down, then turned back to Hylas. 'I am Meritamen, wife of the Hati-aa of the First Province of the Two Lands.'

Hylas heard Pirra's angry hiss and shot her a warning glance. Of course Pirra was angry – this girl's husband had helped the Crows catch Userref – but it would be disastrous to let on that they knew who he was, that might lead her to Nebetku, and the dagger.

'Why did you bring us here?' barked Pirra in Akean.

Again the girl looked askance at her, as if she was a slave who'd spoken out of turn. Again she spoke only to Hylas. 'What is your name?'

'Flea,' he replied.

Her full lips twisted in amusement. 'Is that your real name?'

'No. Why did you help us get away, then tie us up and bring us here?'

'Why should I not help you? You saved my little sister.'

The child emerged from behind her skirts and stared up at him with her mouth open. She too seemed fascinated by his hair.

'My sister is very spoilt and very disobedient,' Meritamen said fondly. 'She begged to come and see the barbarian who saved her from the cobra. How did you know it was there?'

Again, Hylas shrugged. 'I just did.'

'But how? My sister says you threw your knife the moment *before* the snake appeared.'

He didn't reply.

She moved closer.

She wore an ankle-length dress of white linen so fine it was almost sheer, netted with tiny turquoise beads that shimmered at her every move. A sash of silvered calfskin cinched her narrow waist, and on her upper arms, gold rings pressed into her smooth brown flesh. Across her neck and shoulders lay a broad collar banded with red chalcedony and rows of living green leaves: mint, willow, and the evergreen plant Egyptians call *isd*.

Pirra said something, but Hylas didn't take it in. He felt breathless and hot. He tried to swallow, but his throat had closed.

The Egyptian girl's glossy black hair was a mass of tiny braids down her back, gathered in two bunches on either side of her face. Her features were as regular as a statue's: large slanted dark eyes outlined in black, the lids an iridescent green. Lips hennaed a rich, troubling red. And yet, behind the paint, it was a girl who gazed up at him: dauntingly pretty, but not entirely sure of herself.

'Why do you fear Lord Tel-amon?' she said softly.

He cleared his throat. 'I don't.'

'Then you won't mind if I tell him that you're here.'

He didn't reply.

Meritamen leant closer. He caught the spicy scent of her skin. Her breath heated his face as she stood on tiptoe and whispered in his ear: 'I know about the dagger.'

Not a muscle moved in Hylas' face.

'I know about the dagger,' repeated the Egyptian girl. She stood gazing up at him. Far too close. Why did she have to stand so close? Pirra hated her. She was acutely aware of her own dusty, dishevelled appearance.

'I don't know what you mean,' Hylas said at last.

'Yes you do,' said Meritamen. 'An outsider with yellow hair: that's what Lord Tel-amon said. And a Keftian girl with a scar.'

Pirra glared at her.

'He said you are the enemies of his kin,' Meritamen went on, her eyes never leaving Hylas'. 'He said you are after his dagger.'

'Then why are you helping us escape?' broke in Pirra.

'Because you saved my sister,' the girl told Hylas. 'Because Lord Tel-amon hates you – and because I hate him.'

'She's lying,' said Pirra. 'This is just a trick to make us talk.'

'I will get you safely out of Pa-Sobek,' the girl told Hylas, as if Pirra hadn't spoken. 'Kerasher must not hear of this, it will be as if it never happened. If you are caught, you will be on your own. So. You will leave now and never come back.'

'We can't do that,' said Hylas and Pirra together.

Meritamen drew herself up. 'I must have the dagger,' she said coldly. 'I must give it to Lord Tel-amon by the dawn of the First Drop – that is the day after tomorrow.'

'Why?' said Hylas.

The Egyptian girl swallowed. 'I must save my family from the wrath of the Perao.'

Pirra studied her face. Then she laughed. 'You don't know where it is!'

'But I know that Nebetku has it,' the girl shot back, 'and he will give it to me soon!'

A horrified silence. *She knows about Nebetku*, thought Pirra. She didn't dare meet Hylas' eyes.

Meritamen saw their stricken expressions, and nodded. 'Oh yes, I've known Nebetku all my life. He was kind to me when I was little. But I haven't told Lord Tel-amon about him. I'm not so wicked that I'd let them torture a dying man. Lord Tel-amon doesn't even know that the thief who stole his dagger *had* a brother.'

This was too much for Pirra. 'Userref was no thief!' she shouted. 'He never did anything but good – and yet you stood by like a coward and let the Crows hound him to death!'

'I am not a coward!' retorted the girl.

'Pirra, please!' Hylas turned to Meritamen. 'We won't tell you where the dagger is, if that's what you're after.'

Meritamen brushed that aside. 'You saved my sister, so I will save you from the barbarians – but I do not *need* you to tell me where is this dagger! I have already sent word to Nebetku. Soon he will *give* me the dagger!'

'He'll never do that,' snarled Pirra.

'Yes he will,' said Meritamen with infuriating calm. 'He has no choice.'

They were on the River again, their arms bound, although less tightly, being rowed across by a boatman who sat with his back to them, silent and faceless in a hooded robe.

It was dark, and ahead of them, the East Bank was alive with torchlight. The clamour of flutes and the smell of roasting meat drifted over the water. The *heb* would go on all night.

Pirra shifted uncomfortably and flexed her shoulders. She saw Hylas glance at the water, as if weighing the odds of swimming for it. She shot him a warning look and shook her head. *Don't be mad, you'd drown!*

'I wouldn't try it,' the boatman said in Egyptian. 'Lots of crocodiles on that sandbank over there.'

Suddenly, Pirra noticed that instead of taking the long route across, which avoided the tricky currents and the rocks, the boatman was in fact turning back towards the West Bank. He steered the boat past a bend, and the lights of the *heb* blinked out.

'What's happening?' said Hylas.

'Where are you taking us?' Pirra cried in Egyptian.

'You'll see,' muttered the boatman. His voice was oddly familiar.

'The Lady Meritamen said we are not to be harmed,' said Pirra.

'I don't work for the Lady Meritamen.' The boatman threw back his hood, and Pirra saw his strange, gaunt young face and his wispy grey hair. '*Herihor*,' she said in astonishment.

'You're to come with me,' he said. 'Nebetku needs your help.'

19

This time, Nebetku wasn't in the *shabti* work-shop, but in a long low house packed with scrolls of papyrus. Pirra saw newly washed sheets of it hanging to dry, and reed pens and pallets blotched with red and black ink.

Pellets of sweet resin were burning in a small clay brazier; the smell was oddly familiar. Near it stood a little plaster god with the head of an ibis. Pirra recognized it as Tjehuti, Lord of Time and God of Knowledge – and of scribes. They were in Nebetku's own workshop.

He lay on a mat with his neck on a headrest. Rensi the dwarf sat beside him. Pirra was shocked. If Nebetku had been ill before, he was now clearly dying. His sunken eyes darted, seeking peace and finding none. 'This is *your* doing,' he told her in Egyptian. 'You killed him – and now this!'

'Speak Akean,' growled Hylas.

'Get him out,' Nebetku told Rensi. He broke into a frenzy of coughing. The dwarf handed him a blood-spattered rag which he pressed to his mouth.

'If he's telling me to go,' said Hylas, 'I won't. I'm sick of being pushed around. If he wants our help, he talks to us both.'

Nebetku laboured for breath. 'The Lady Merita-men,' he said in Akean, 'is clever. Her spies couldn't discover where I hid the dagger – so they found a way to make me give it up. The night before we put User-ref in his tomb, I kept watch over his body in Herihor's workshop. One of her spies put a potion in my beer, and while I slept . . .' His face worked. 'Her spy entered the workshop and stole the *peret em heru* – the Spells for Coming Forth by Day – from my brother's coffin. In its place the spy left a blank scroll. I found out today, when she sent me word.'

'What does this mean?' asked Hylas.

'I forget you know nothing,' panted Nebetku. 'When an Egyptian dies, his spirit makes the perilous journey through the Duat – the world of the Dead. In the Hall of Two Truths, his heart is weighed against the Feather of *Maat*, and he must answer the questions of the Forty-Two Judges. Only with the Spells for Coming Forth by Day can he pass the trials of the Duat and reach the blessed place under the Sun – the Place of Reeds – where the crops never fail and the cattle are always fat – and everyone is young and healthy . . .'

Weakly, he gestured at the scrolls stacked from floor to roof beam. 'All these are *peret em heru*. I've spent my life writing the Spells, over and over, for merchants, priests, temple singers . . . And yet my own brother will stand before the Judges with blank papyrus!' His burning gaze sought Pirra's. 'You ask what this means. It means his spirit will be eaten by the Devourer. It means he will be *mutu* – cursed – he will suffer the Second Death and cease to be. It means that when I reach the Place of Reeds, he will not be there! I will never see him again!' He burst into painful, wrenching sobs.

Rensi put a comforting hand on his shoulder. Heri-hor fluttered his bony fingers, then added more resin to the brazier, releasing more scented smoke.

Pirra remembered it now: Userref used to burn it to cheer her up. She thought of his spirit trapped in the tomb, or lost in the Duat, or perhaps already standing before the Judges, in terror of the Devourer . . .

Nebetku gave a ghastly, rattling laugh. 'If only that spy had known that the dagger was inside the *coffin*! He could have stolen it while I slept, and left my poor brother in peace!'

'So why do you need us?' Hylas said impatiently. 'Why can't you just open the tomb and swap the scrolls?'

Nebetku shot him a look. 'Because the Hati-aa's guards won't let us! The Lady Meritamen has let it be known that there are tomb-robbers about, and has set a watch on the Houses of Eternity. Today at the *heb*, she sent me word: "*Bring me the dagger and I will call off the guards, so that you may restore the Spells to your brother. If not . . .*' His lips trembled. '*If not, he will suffer the Second Death.*"'

'Then why not tell her the dagger's in the tomb?' said Hylas. 'She can send in her men and they can get it –'

'*Never!*' gasped Nebetku. 'My ancestors have kept our tomb secret for generations – and so it must remain! I will not be the one to endanger their eternal rest!'

'Then what can we do?' cried Pirra.

Clumsily, Nebetku wiped his lips with the bloody rag. 'There is a way for someone to get inside without the guards knowing.'

'Why do you want us to do it?' said Hylas. 'Why not Herihor or Rensi?'

'They have duties at the *heb*, their absence would be noted. Besides . . .' The emaciated features hardened. 'To disturb the peace of the ancestors – why should my friends risk their souls when it was you who killed him? Let *you* put it right!'

'What do we get out of it?' retorted Hylas.

'If you replace the Spells and save my brother's spirit, you can take your filthy dagger from his coffin.'

Pirra felt sick. Meritamen had been clever. But then, she was desperate. She would stop at nothing to protect her family from the wrath of the Perao, even it meant dooming Userref's spirit for eternity.

Hylas was running his thumb along his lower lip. 'What about Meritamen? She needs the dagger. If she doesn't get it, she'll come after you.'

The dying man snorted. 'Let her! Once I know Userref's *ba* is safe, I'll have nothing to fear. Soon I will be dead. I will become a *sah*, a Wrapped One. I will join my brother in our tomb, and when I too have journeyed through the Duat, we will be together in the Place of Reeds for eternity.'

Rensi gulped and pinched the bridge of his nose. Herihor shifted unhappily from foot to foot.

Hylas made to speak, but Pirra got in first. 'I'll do it. I'll go into the tomb.'

'We'll go together,' said Hylas.

'No,' said Nebetku. 'There is space only for one.'

'Then it has to be me,' said Pirra. 'Yes it does, Hylas. It's my fault he died, it's up to me to save his spirit.'

He looked at her. 'Pirra. You get panicky in a *cave*. You couldn't stand being shut up in a tomb, you'd go mad! I could handle it; when I was a slave, I spent ages down the mines.'

'But there might be ghosts,' protested Pirra.

'I haven't seen a single ghost since I've been in Egypt,' he said.

'They are all at peace,' put in Nebetku, 'for in Egypt we know the proper rites. All except my poor brother.' He glanced at Pirra. 'The boy will go in the tomb. I have a role for you, too.'

'Well, then,' said Hylas. 'Tell us what to do.'

———

'Two moons ago,' said Nebetku, 'one of the sacred crocodiles died.'

'A good omen for the Flood,' Herihor said in Egyptian. 'I have embalmed it, so it can take its place in the *heb*.'

'Tomorrow is the Eve of the First Drop,' Nebetku went on in Akean. 'The *heb* will come to the West

Bank, and the sacred crocodile will be buried in the tomb of the animals – you do not need to know where this is, let us call it simply the Crocodile Tomb.' He struggled for breath.

'Long ago, my ancestors were embalmers of animals. They knew the Crocodile Tomb well, all its twisting tunnels. When they fell out of favour with the great ones, they sought a secret place to conceal their dead. So from a passage in the Crocodile Tomb, they dug a secret tunnel. This is the only way to reach the place where Userref is buried: by the hidden tunnel that leads from the Crocodile Tomb to that of my ancestors.'

Even thinking about it made Pirra want to throw up, but Hylas seemed alarmingly untroubled.

'Rensi and Herihor,' said the sick man, 'are making space for you to lie inside the coffin of the sacred crocodile.'

'*What?*' cried Pirra. 'You want to put him in a *coffin?*'

'Pirra it's all right,' said Hylas.

'This is very dangerous for the crocodile,' said Herihor in Egyptian, 'that barbarian is unclean!'

Luckily, Hylas didn't understand.

'Inside the coffin,' Nebetku went on, 'you will be part of the procession, but no one will know you are there. You will be carried into the Crocodile Tomb and sealed inside –'

'No!' said Pirra.

'– at night when the *heb* is gone, you will crawl through the tunnel to *our* tomb; that is, to Userref's tomb. You will replace the Spells in his coffin and remove the cursed dagger for which he died. You will then crawl back through the tunnel, into the Crocodile Tomb, where you will be let out.'

'How?' said Pirra. 'You said the Crocodile Tomb will be sealed.'

Nebetku met her eyes. 'The Lady Meritamen often visits the West Bank to pray for the health of the Hati-aa. Where she prays, at the tomb of his ancestors, is not far from the entrance to the Crocodile Tomb. In the dark, if you dressed like her, the guards would believe you *were* her . . . They would let you through. Then you could let the barbarian out.'

'Oh, no,' said Hylas, 'that's far too dangerous –'

'It could work,' said Pirra.

'It *must* work,' said Nebetku.

'Come,' Rensi said briskly in Egyptian. 'We need to measure the barbarian for the coffin.'

The smell in Herihor's embalming workshops was a nauseating mix of boiled oxhide, resin and decay, but

Herihor took a deep sniff and smiled. 'Behold my House of Rebirth. Don't touch *anything.*'

His workshops were set apart from the others and hidden behind high walls. They were the cleanest rooms Pirra had ever seen. Everything gleamed: copper sieves, hooks, tongs, tweezers, knives of flint and obsidian, and everything was precisely aligned: baskets of chopped straw, vats of sacred salt, jars of gums and spices, rolls of bandages . . .

Pirra stared at a spotless limestone slab on a trestle. It was slightly tilted, with drainage grooves and a jar underneath, to catch drips.

'I like things *clean,*' said Herihor, rubbing his bony hands. He glanced at Pirra in distaste. 'The living are so dirty.'

Hylas was gazing around him. 'These are animals.'

'Don't touch!' cried Herihor.

Dangling from the roofbeams – presumably to protect them from mice – were creatures so deftly bandaged that Pirra could tell at once what they were: baboons, cats, fish, even something that looked worryingly like a falcon. The only thing she didn't recognize was a row of tiny neat balls, the size of plums.

Rensi chuckled. 'Bees. Not many embalmers can do those.'

Herihor led them into a smaller workshop occupied by two trestles. On one lay the unmistakable form of a large bandaged crocodile with a greenstone scarab between its eye-bumps. On the other, a long tapered coffin.

'Hylas cannot go in that,' Pirra said flatly.

'I'll manage,' he said. But he'd gone pale.

The coffin was wooden, painted inside and out with stripes to look like bandages, the stripes filled in with brightly coloured writing. Beside it lay a large half-painted wooden lid. Pirra saw two spreading wings – but no air-holes. 'How will he breathe?' she demanded.

Herihor blinked, as if that hadn't occurred to him.

'We'll bore holes,' Rensi said hastily. 'We haven't finished it yet, we're still making it. See how it's higher? That's to leave room for the barbarian.'

'The main thing,' said Herihor, 'is to keep him separate from the Wrapped One. He must be washed, purged and fumigated, and I'll put a mat underneath with purifying herbs, to keep his unclean flesh from sullying the Wrapped One.'

All this was spoken in Egyptian. When Pirra translated for Hylas, he was too startled to be offended. 'Isn't it the dead crocodile who'll be sullying *me*?'

Herihor guessed his meaning. 'It's the *living* who are unclean!' Lovingly, he passed his bony fingers over the crocodile, taking care not to touch it. 'I remove all imperfections,' he said fervently. 'The guts, the worthless brain . . . I cleanse the flesh in wine and spices till it's light and pure as the sands of the *deshret* – I leave nothing inside but the hard dry heart. I *rescue* the dead, I make them *perfect*!'

Rensi cast his friend an affectionate glance. 'Herihor is the master. There is no better embalmer in all Pa-Sobek.'

Pirra was staring at the coffin, picturing Hylas inside.

He touched her arm. 'I'll be all right.'

She shook her head. 'You don't understand how dangerous this is. You see all this writing? The little painted signs? The whole point of them is to create what they describe. Hylas, they're going to come alive in the tomb!'

He swallowed.

'That's why the dangerous ones are missing bits,' she said. 'You see how they've left the claws off the vultures and the sting off the scorpions? Cut off the snakes' tails, put little red spears through the crocodile signs? That's to stop them doing harm!'

'Well then, there's no problem,' he said defensively.

'But you don't know if it'll *work*!' she burst out. 'No one knows!'

'I'll be all right,' he repeated, as if to convince himself. He forced a laugh. 'I mean, Pirra: an Egyptian tomb with an Outsider in it? Their gods won't *let* me stay in there for long, they'll spit me out!'

'That,' she said, 'is what I'm afraid of.'

20

The *heb* had lasted most of the night, and the Hati-aa's residence was still slumbering when Telamon was woken by the braying of a donkey. Too much wine had given him a pounding head, and he was furious with himself for losing Meritamen in the crowd. That was a mistake a boy would make, not a man.

Stumbling out of his quarters, he staggered outside to get some air.

Mist hazed the River, and over on the West Bank, the cliffs were flushed dark pink in the rising Sun. Around him, the outdoor slaves were preparing for the second day of the *heb*. Brewers stirred beer-vats, washerwomen pounded wet linen. A sleepy maidservant sprinkled water to settle the dust, and another yawned as she scattered grain in the duck-pen. The smell of baking bread made Telamon queasy.

How am I ever going to find the dagger? he wondered. What would Pharax do? Or Koronos?

It struck him that he hadn't asked himself what his father would do. But compared to his kinsmen, Thestor was weak. He was kind, too, and at Mycenae, Telamon had learnt that kindness didn't work. Men like Pharax and Koronos got respect because they were feared.

Children were playing near the fig orchards: boys stick-fighting, girls hunched over a game of knuckle bones. Telamon spotted Meritamen's little sister, squatting near some beehives with her cat sprawled beside her. He was pleased to see that Kerasher had set one of his slaves to watch the child; but it irked him to remember that it was Alekto who had asked Kerasher to arrange this. Alekto takes too much upon herself, thought Telamon. She needs to understand that *I* am the leader.

The little girl was busy scolding a wooden doll with straggly date-fibre hair. Something about the child's scowl reminded Telamon sharply of Issi, Hylas' sister. Telamon had liked Issi, and she'd worshipped him – before everything had gone wrong.

The beekeeper was wafting a pot of burning cattle

dung around the hives, to calm them. They were big clay cylinders stacked on top of each other in the shade of a fig tree, and around them, bees came and went with their usual mysterious certainty.

Suddenly, Telamon was back home on Mount Lykas, on that summer's day when he and Hylas and Issi had tracked the wild bees. It had been Hylas' idea. He'd found a pool where bees came to drink, and the three of them had darted about, flicking powdered red ochre on as many bees as they could, then following the marked ones back to their nest. Well, that was the idea. It had turned into an uproarious race through the forest: 'This way!' 'No don't be an idiot, it's over *here*!'

Eventually, Telamon had spotted the bees' nest half-way up the trunk of an old pine. They'd woken a smoky fire beneath it to calm the bees: Hylas teasing Issi about being scared, she hotly denying it, Telamon secretly anxious and trying not to show it. He and Hylas had taken turns to stand on each other's shoulders and try to reach the nest with a knife tied to a stick. Hylas had managed to sever a honeycomb. He'd yelled at Issi to catch it and she'd missed, and blamed him for bad throwing. Then the three of them had huddled together, counting their bee-stings and cramming honeycomb in their mouths. The *taste* of it: that astonishing sweetness. Like eating sunshine.

The little girl's voice wrenched Telamon back to the present. He was angry with himself. You're a man now, all that's in the past. Burn it. Scorch it from your mind for ever. Be more like Koronos.

The child had stopped scolding her doll, and was making a small clay snake slither menacingly towards it.

Some impulse or maybe some god made Telamon summon Kerasher's slave and have him translate what the child was saying.

'If you wish, my lord,' said the startled slave. 'She says: "And then the cobra slithered towards the little girl . . . but suddenly – *wsh!* – the yellow-haired stranger threw his knife, and –'

'She said *what*?' snapped Telamon.

Nervously, the slave repeated it.

A cold wave washed over Telamon. 'The yellow-haired stranger. You're sure she said that.'

The slave nodded. 'She keeps saying it.' He smiled. 'Children are like that –'

'The yellow-haired stranger,' said a woman's voice behind Telamon. His skin prickled with loathing.

Alekto looked very fresh and cool in her long sleeveless dress of green and black silk, with gilded sandals on her hennaed feet. 'Well *done*, nephew,' she said with her mocking smile. 'This almost makes up for losing sight of the girl at the *heb*.'

Telamon's cheeks flamed. 'I hear you killed another peasant yesterday.'

She laughed. 'I can't help it if they're weak.'

'Alekto,' Telamon said sharply. 'Go back inside. I'll question the child alone.'

She tilted her lovely head. 'Oh, nephew, that's not –'

'My name is Telamon,' he said in a tone that made her blink. 'Go back inside.'

Her dark eyes flashed, but she turned, and went back inside.

It worked, thought Telamon. It actually worked.

Meritamen's little sister had stopped playing and was staring up at him. Telamon strode towards her. She scrambled to her feet and placed herself protectively between him and her cat. Behind her, the boys stopped stick-fighting and ran away. The girls gathered up their knuckle-bones and followed.

With a new sense of confidence, Telamon made Kerasher's slave ask the child in Egyptian where she'd seen the stranger with the yellow hair.

The little girl went on staring at him with round dark eyes.

Telamon had the slave repeat the question.

Still nothing.

Meritamen emerged from the house and came hurrying over.

Telamon knew then that the gods were indeed on his side. They had ensured that he learnt what the child had seen, and now they'd sent him her sister.

Dismissing the slave, he smiled down at Meritamen. 'You've been lying to me,' he said pleasantly.

She flinched. 'No.' But he could see the blood beating in her throat.

'Oh, yes,' he replied. 'Hylas the Outsider is here in Pa-Sobek. Don't deny it, your sister saw him. I take it the Keftian girl with the scar is here too.' He read the answer in her face. 'Where are they?'

'I don't know.'

'I don't believe you.'

She lifted her chin defiantly. 'It is not for you to speak in such a way to the wife of the Hati-aa. Soon I will have your dagger for you. Then you can go back to your own land.'

Again Telamon smiled. 'But I want the Outsider too. You have spies. You must know where they are.'

'I did, but someone helped them get away.'

'Indeed.' Telamon placed his hand on the little sister's shaven head. He felt the soft downy fuzz, and beneath it, the fragile skull.

Meritamen's eyes widened as he squeezed the child's temples: gently, just making a point. 'Pretty child,' he murmured. 'The Lady Alekto likes her *very* much.'

The blood drained from Meritamen's lips.

'I wouldn't want anything to happen to her,' Telamon went on. 'But you know how at times the Lady Alekto goes too far.'

'You wouldn't dare touch her,' said Meritamen.

'I have the favour of the Perao,' replied Telamon. 'You don't know what I would dare to do.'

Her throat worked, as if she was trying to swallow. 'They're on the West Bank. That's all I know, I swear!'

Telamon gazed across the River at the tall cliffs, tawny now that the Sun had risen, and pocked with man-made caves.

And suddenly, he *knew*. 'The dagger,' he said. 'It's in a *tomb*.'

21

They slept on rush mats in Rensi's *shabti* work-shop. Pirra dreamt Hylas was trapped in a tomb, screaming to be let out, while she tried frantically to find him.

She woke around midnight to see him sitting up in the dark. 'I'll be back soon,' he whispered. 'I need to make sure Havoc's all right.'

When she woke again he'd returned, smelling of lions and the desert. It was nearly dawn. Today, the *heb* would reach the West Bank, and the crocodile coffin – with him inside – would be carried to its tomb. Pirra asked when it would start, and he said not till afternoon, but Herihor needed him before then, to be purified. He made a face. She gave him a strained smile.

Rensi came in with his wife Berenib, a plump motherly woman, who towered over her husband. She'd brought fried bean cakes and oniony beer: Hylas wolfed his, but Pirra had to force hers down. Dread lay on her stomach like a stone.

Rensi took Hylas away, and Berenib hustled Pirra off to make a start on her disguise. Noticing Pirra's stricken face, she gave her a little pat. 'Don't worry, you'll see your lion-haired barbarian before the *heb*.'

Until now, Pirra had only seen the West Bank by night. This morning it was heaving, everyone preparing for the procession. Berenib said there were in fact *two* villages: Tjebu, where 'the lower workers' lived – tomb-diggers, reed-cutters, water-carriers, peasants, fishermen – and Gesa, for craftsmen such as her husband. She was clearly proud of the difference.

The *shabti*-maker lived in a small mudbrick house with his wife, their three children and their pet ibis. To make room for Pirra, all but the ibis had been sent away. Pirra found it quite comforting to let Berenib take over. It took her mind off what was going to happen to Hylas.

'First, we need to get you *clean*,' muttered Berenib. She gave Pirra a reed toothbrush and papyrus-root paste, then the juice of sycomore figs to sweeten her breath. A body scrub with sacred salt was next, a thorough rinse, pellets of carob seed and incense rubbed under her arms, and finally Berenib's 'special mixture' of goosefat and honey, to smooth her skin. (Berenib called most things her 'special mixture', and insisted on telling Pirra what went into each one.)

To add lustre to her hair, there was a 'special lotion' of sesame oil and juniper, then Berenib spent ages making lots of tiny plaits, with two bunches at the front, woven with purple feathers and white lotus flowers. Her 'special perfume' was a small pat of river-horse fat scented with jasmine. She wanted to put it on Pirra's parting, where it would slowly melt, but Pirra refused. Berenib insisted. Pirra gave in.

After hennaing Pirra's hands and feet, she selected a pair of finely woven reed sandals, then helped her into a narrow sheath of pleated white linen with scarlet straps, a yellow fringe that brushed her ankles, and a beaded blue sash at the waist. Instead of real jewels, there were bronze wrist-cuffs, anklets, and copper hoops for her ears, with a heavy collar of green jasper that covered her breasts, and was counter-balanced at the back by a length of turquoise beads: Berenib called this a *menit*.

There was a tussle over the rawhide cuff on Pirra's

forearm, which Berenib won: the cuff came off. But Pirra kept her Keftian necklace tied round her waist under her dress; and she strapped her knife to her shin.

When at last she was dressed, she tried a few steps – and nearly fell over. The narrow skirts hobbled her, and the sandals were so slippery she knew they'd never been worn. 'Is all this yours?' she asked.

Berenib's laugh made her chins wobble. 'Oh, I'd never fit a dress that size! I borrowed everything from our stores.'

'What stores?'

Berenib seemed disconcerted. 'Well . . . Some people dress their Blessed Ones before they bring them, but others leave it to us.'

'Oh,' said Pirra. She'd been given clothes for the dead.

Berenib gave her another little pat. 'Have some of my special calming potion. Grated lotus root in pomegranate wine, never been know to fail. Now sit still while I do your face.'

By mid-afternoon the West Bank was at fever pitch, so it was easy for Berenib and Pirra, suitably veiled, to reach Nebetku's workshop without being noticed. There Berenib left her. Pirra was dismayed to find

Nebetku, but not Hylas. All her dread came rushing back. 'Where is he?' she cried.

'With Herihor, being purified,' said Nebetku.

'But he will come back? I mean – before the coffin?'

'He will. Sit. Wait with me.' He indicated a rush mat near his.

Awkward in her new clothes, Pirra knelt.

Nebetku seemed a little better today, perhaps because he now had hope for his brother's spirit. Pirra noticed that he'd placed a dish of water in a corner, and Echo was splashing in it. The falcon seemed more subdued than usual; maybe she'd sensed Pirra's apprehension.

Nebetku coughed and wiped his lips, and studied her. 'Berenib did well. In the dark, you could pass for the Lady Meriramen.'

'I'll have to do more than that, I'll have to give orders in Egyptian that will fool the guards.'

'Rensi will help . . . He and Herihor will go with you as your slaves. The guards would think it odd if you went alone.'

'Good.' But she still felt hollow with dread.

'I made this for you.' Nebetku held out a strip of papyrus. Wind it round your belt, for luck. I made another for the barbarian.'

The papyrus was painted with sacred signs. Pirra recognized a few. A bee, a pot and the Sun meant 'honey', while a tiny kneeling man with his arms tied behind meant 'enemy', or 'barbarian'. All were written in red: the colour of danger.

'This is a spell,' Pirra said in a low voice.

Nebetku blinked. 'How is it you know the *medu netjer?*'

'I don't, just a few signs. Userref taught me . . .' She broke off, remembering lessons in the House of the Goddess. *Never let your pen hand touch the papyrus, Pirra . . . And don't look at the tip, look at where you want it to go . . .*

'I always wanted to draw birds,' she said shakily. 'I used to get cross because my owls didn't look like owls. Userref said birds are the hardest. "Start with the breast," he'd tell me, "because that's where its mind is, then down to the feet, then the tail, and the rest. Do the beak last: pull it out from the ink with a little flick. That's when it becomes a bird . . ."'

Nebetku tried to swallow. 'I told him that. I didn't think he remembered.'

Echo finished her bath and began tidying her feathers.

'He remembered everything,' said Pirra. 'He taught me how to care for falcons, too. He said you taught him that. He never stopped missing you, or wanting to go home.'

Tears were sliding down Nebetku's wasted cheeks.

Pirra willed herself not to cry. No sense in Berenib having to repaint her face. 'I have to ask you something. If your tomb is so secret, why don't you mind telling Hylas how to find it?'

He wiped his face with his fingers. 'He asked me that too.'

'So why is it? Don't you expect him to survive?'

'Of course I do, I need him to replace the Spells.'

'And afterwards? How will he survive a tomb full of curses and *shabtis* and ghosts?'

'He will have enough air until about midnight. If he gets out by then, he lives. If not . . .'

'What then?'

He coughed and went on coughing. 'All I care about,' he panted, 'is saving my brother's *ba*. I have no strength for anything else.'

Outside, a flock of crows settled raucously in a tree. Echo flew off to chase them away.

All this suffering, thought Pirra, because of the Crows.

She thought of Telamon at the *heb*: a handsome warrior now, but secretly terrified that he wasn't enough of a man to be a leader. And she thought of

Alekto, with her perfect face and her beautiful black eyes, as empty of humanity as two holes cut in marble.

Pirra's grief hardened to anger, and she made a silent promise to Userref: *Whatever happens, your death will be avenged.*

To Nebetku she said: 'I need you to help me make another spell.'

Herihor had returned Hylas' knife, and Hylas had persuaded him (with Nebetku translating) to give him *two* sheaths: one for his own knife, strapped to his arm like Kem's, and another at his belt, to hold the dagger of Koronos.

The embalmer had gone to fetch them, leaving Hylas alone in the outer workshop, when Pirra appeared in the doorway.

He was stunned. She looked highborn and haughtily beautiful. But then, he reminded himself, she *is* highborn. Her disguise works because she was born to it.

Her face was a painted stillness, her eyelids green, her eyes thickly rimmed with black, with a short line descending from her lower lids, like a falcon's teardrop. He guessed she'd done that herself, to give her courage.

'How did you get on with Herihor?' she said quietly.

He glanced down at the new kilt which the embalmer had forced him into. His skin was still burning from being scrubbed all over. 'Not that good. He wanted to shave me all over. We settled for plaiting my hair.' He gave her a lopsided smile.

She didn't smile back. 'All those braids. You look like a warrior.'

'Well I'm not.'

'Hylas, I need you to do something for me.' She held out Userref's *wedjat* amulet. 'Put this in his coffin. He thought I was dead. Tell him I'm not and I miss him. Tell him – to be at peace.'

'I will.' He wanted to say something more: to tell her that if this didn't work, not to try and find his body. Just run away, Rensi and Herihor would look after her . . . Instead he blurted out, 'You look good, Pirra. You'll have no trouble getting past the guards.'

Her mouth twisted. 'Do I look like her?'

He thought she looked better than Meritamen, but Pirra mistook his hesitation, and put her hand to her scar.

'Forget about your scar,' he told her. 'It doesn't matter. The Moon has scars, but it's still beautiful.'

Pirra blinked. Then she gave an uncertain smile, as if she couldn't quite believe what he'd just said.

At that moment, Rensi and Herihor appeared in the doorway. Hurriedly, Pirra pressed a strip of papyrus into Hylas' palm and closed his fingers over it. 'Nebetku made this for you. Wear it as a headband to protect you.'

He nodded but couldn't speak.

Herihor said something in Egyptian, and Pirra's eyes widened. 'It's time,' she said.

The haze from Berenib's calming potion cleared, and Hylas woke up.

He heard muffled flutes and wailing. The *heb* was still outside the tomb. He had to stay where he was.

He was lying in darkness so thick he could taste it. The heat was stifling, his breath horribly loud, the lid of the coffin almost touching his nose. Rensi had bored airholes, hidden by garlands heaped on top. It didn't feel as if he'd made enough.

The coffin was so narrow Hylas couldn't move: his legs were clamped together, his arms pressed to his sides. Against his thigh lay Nebetku's scroll of spells. He tried to concentrate on that.

It didn't work. The mat on which he lay was scratchy with myrtle, strewn by Herihor to prevent him defiling what was beneath. Under the mat, garlands of blue lotus released their overpowering scent, and from beneath came the sour tang of the Wrapped One: the sacred crocodile waiting to begin its journey to the Duat.

Fighting panic, Hylas prayed that the procession would leave now, so that he could climb out. Nebetku had said to listen for the sound of breaking pots: smashing the jars of the funeral feast meant the rites were over, and the tomb would be sealed.

All he heard were more wails and muffled chants. He couldn't stand it much longer.

'*Don't* climb out too soon,' Nebetku had warned. 'They will hear you, and all will be over!'

To distract himself, Hylas went over the plan of the Crocodile Tomb in his head. Nebetku had scratched it in sand, then swiftly smoothed it out. 'The black cat marks the opening to the tunnel. Once through it, you will be in the chamber of my ancestors. Beyond that is the burial chamber where my brother lies.' He'd paused. 'The tunnel might be a problem, your shoulders are broader than an Egyptian's. Try not to get stuck . . .'

Stuck? In a tunnel deep underground in a sealed tomb?

Stop it, Hylas. Think about afterwards, when you've swapped the scrolls, got the dagger, and Pirra has let you out . . .

A sharp pain in his temples made him wince. Lights flickered behind his eyes. The veil shrouding the world of the spirits was blowing aside. Well, of course. He was inside a tomb.

Something tickled his ankle. A spider? An ant?

Something else touched his knee: a feather-light scratch of tiny claws.

Spiders and ants don't have claws. He thought of the little sacred signs that covered the inside of the coffin, and his heart began to pound. *They're going to come alive in the tomb . . .*

In Itineb's village, Pirra had shown him a sign of a trussed duck waiting to be killed: she'd said it meant fear. At the time, he'd laughed. He wasn't laughing now.

He heard faint scrabblings and gnawings. His hands brushed the sides of the coffin. Things skittered away from his fingers. He thought of tiny vipers and wasps, vultures and knives and bodiless feet and hands, *scorpions . . .*

As he lay battling panic, the whole coffin lurched.

No – not the coffin itself: what lay within. Beneath the myrtle-strewn mat and the crushed lotus, the Wrapped One itself was beginning to move.

Rigid with horror, Hylas felt the snakelike swish of its great tail undulate from side to side. The crocodile was setting off on its final journey. It was swimming upriver to the Duat.

And taking him with it.

22

It was dark by the time the *heb* came down from the cliffs and headed back across the River – and Pirra was sick with dread. No one really knew if Hylas would have enough air.

Rensi and Herihor appeared, dressed as her slaves: Rensi without his wig, Herihor having shaved off his grey hair; he looked more like a skeleton than ever. Nebetku watched from his workshop as they set off for the Houses of Eternity.

'I'll do the talking,' muttered Rensi. 'The guards will expect this. All you need to do is confirm what I tell them, just say: "It is so."'

'It is so,' repeated Pirra. But surely the guards would hear that she wasn't the Hati-aa's wife?

Rensi moved fast on his short legs, and Herihor

loped beside him, carrying the offerings 'the Lady Meritamen' was taking to her family tomb: a basket of pomegranates and sycomore figs, a jar of wine and a big nodding fan of lotus flowers. Pirra hissed at them to slow down. She couldn't stride in her narrow dress, and her sandals were still slippery, even though she'd roughened the soles with grit.

Rensi led them by shadowy back ways, past fields of stubble. He hadn't told Pirra the whereabouts of the Crocodile Tomb, and she didn't ask now. Better she didn't know, in case she was caught.

Behind her lay the dark sprawl of the workshops, and the pale glimmer of the Hati-aa's stables. To her left, a gorge cut through the hills: she heard the sinister cackle of hyaenas out in the desert. To her right, the villages of Tjebu and Gesa were bright with cooking fires. Across the River, more fires: she caught the distant music of the *heb*. It would go on for another seven days, until the Flood was well under way.

The Moon rose. They left the fields and climbed a rocky hill, the path snaking up towards the cliffs. The ground on either side was pocked with hollows, some with little clay platters and dishes of water and bread.

'The graves of the poor,' murmured Herihor. 'A hole in the sand and the body wrapped in palm-cloth. Ugh!'

'They do their best,' said Rensi.

'Where are the Hati-aa's guards?' said Pirra uneasily.

'Higher up,' said Rensi. 'Nothing to steal down here, so no tomb-robbers, real or imagined.'

As they climbed higher, the tombs became grander: doorways cut into the hillside, and further up, wider ones with terraced courts in front. Some were still being dug; several had carts and baskets of rubble left by tomb builders. Pirra glimpsed lintels carved with sacred signs. On one, a goddess with the head of a cow stretched out Her arms to greet the rising Sun.

Behind one of these doorways lay the Crocodile Tomb. Had Hylas already found his way to Userref's coffin? Or was he lying unconscious, already suffocating?

Herihor had given him a fine linen kilt and a wide red belt. He'd looked good, but Pirra hated that the embalmer had treated him like a Wrapped One, and made him handsome for his coffin.

Not *his* coffin, she corrected herself. It belongs to the crocodile. That small error felt like the worst of omens.

She touched the little pouch tied to her sash. It held the charm Nebetku had helped her make. If all else failed, she would find some way to avenge Userref. But for Hylas it would be too late.

She must have spoken out loud, because Herihor cast her a questioning glance. 'Are you sure you drilled lots of airholes?' she said. 'What if he can't breathe?'

Herihor didn't reply. His concern was for those who *never* breathed: he was far more worried about his crocodile.

Rensi hissed at them to be quiet, it wasn't far now.

They rounded a bend, and there were the guards: six men squatting by a fire beneath a clump of acacias, cooking their evening meal. Pirra smelt beer and onions, saw spears propped against each other and long curved bronze knives. *It is so*, she thought. That's all you've got to say.

Rensi waddled forwards. 'Stand aside for the Lady Meritamen,' he said briskly, 'we bring offerings to the shrine of her ancestors.'

Pirra opened her mouth to confirm the order. Before she could speak, a veiled figure emerged form behind the trees.

'It is so,' said Meritamen.

'Don't speak,' said Meritamen in Akean, 'just listen and remember that a word from me and the guards will take you all.'

Pirra, Rensi and Herihor stood rooted to the spot.

'What do you want?' croaked Pirra.

'You know what I want. Lord Tel-amon believes the dagger is in a tomb. I see from your faces that he is right.'

Swiftly, she ordered the guards to remain at their post, then led Pirra and the others out of earshot. 'We must be quick,' she said in Egyptian. 'Tell me in which tomb the dagger lies.'

'I don't know,' lied Pirra.

'But they do – I can see it.' Sharply, Meritamen addressed Rensi and Herihor. 'Take me there at once!'

They didn't move.

She turned to Pirra. 'You must do this! It's the only way, I'll go in your place and let him out! Oh yes, I know Hy-las is in the tomb, my spy overheard you just now. He seeks the dagger, yes?'

'He'll never give it to you,' said Pirra.

'Can't you understand, I'm trying to help you!'

'*Help?*' spat Pirra. 'Stealing from Userref's coffin? Putting his spirit in danger? You call that help? Why are you doing this? How do I know Telamon isn't already here?'

Meritamen hissed in frustration. 'Hy-las saved my sister's life! Because of this, I wish to save his life – and because I hate Tel-amon! Is that not enough? We must be *quick*! I have kept Tel-amon in Pa-Sobek by telling my boatmen to delay – but that won't work for long! If you do not do as I say, he will catch you and torture it out of you – and by then Hy-las will be dead!'

'You're bluffing,' snarled Pirra. 'You wouldn't let Hylas die.'

Meritamen's chin went up. 'If I don't get the dagger, my family is ruined. I will do what I must. What will you do?'

Pirra hesitated.

Rensi whispered in her ear: 'As long as Userref's *ba* is safe, what matters the dagger? Give us the word and we'll take her to the tomb. We can do it so that she won't know which one it is: that way it stays secret, but we'll get the boy out safe!'

Pirra chewed her lip. Rensi was right. Let Telamon have the dagger, so long as Hylas got out alive.

And yet. What if Meritamen was lying? What if Telamon was already here on the West Bank, ready to follow them to the tomb and kill Hylas the moment he stepped outside?

'*Hurry!*' urged Meritamen. 'Time is running out!'

Pirra looked at her, then slowly nodded. 'You can take my place – but only if you do something for me.'

23

Hylas pushed the lid of the coffin aside and took great heaving gulps of air.

Darkness pressed on him, heavy with incense and offerings already starting to rot. The silence was absolute. Far away in the land of the living, the *heb* had gone.

He scrambled out, feeling tiny things swarming like beetles over his hands. He pictured the *medu netjer* pouring over the sides of the coffin and skittering over the floor. He touched his headband and prayed that Nebetku's spells would protect him.

It was utterly dark, he couldn't see his hand in front of his face. He groped for the lid of the coffin, slid it back in place, stood swaying with Nebetku's scroll in his fist. Where was he? Had the sacred crocodile swum on without him and left him in the tomb? Or was the tomb itself in the Duat?

Nebetku had tried to explain it, but even to him, it was a mystery. 'There are seven parts to a man's spirit, of which his *ka* and his *ba* are only two. The *ka* stays in the tomb. If the *ba* passes the trials of the Duat, it flies out by day and enjoys the Place of Reeds, returning at night.'

Hylas panted in the hot thick air. Silence roared in his ears. 'Light,' he muttered to give himself courage. His voice rang unpleasantly loud.

'Everything you'll need will be in a jar,' Nebetku had told him. 'You'll find it by the tail of the coffin. You'll know the jar by its lid: it will have the head of a baboon.'

It was horrible, feeling in the dark, dreading what he might find. His fingers fumbled jars with different heads: a bird's beak, a jackal's pointed ears. Ah. The blunt muzzle of a baboon.

Beneath his hand, the muzzle bared its teeth in a snarl. Hylas jerked back with a cry. The jar fell with a clatter. When the echoes died, the silence felt alive: as if something had woken.

His heart hammered in his chest as he groped for the jar. He felt inside. Familiar objects steadied him a little: strike-fire, palm-fibre tinder, two torches.

Earlier, Rensi had shown him, so that he'd know what to expect. Each torch was twisted canvas, stiffened between two lathes and soaked in linseed oil. 'Tomb-painters' torches,' the dwarf had explained through Nebetku. 'They salt the oil, so that it won't smoke and leave marks on the paintings. Whatever you do, *don't* drop it. If you start a fire in there, that's the end.'

Hylas' hands were shaking so hard he nearly dropped the strike-fire, but at last he persuaded a spark to take. Light flared. Shadows skittered away as the *medu netjer* fled for the dark. Hylas twisted round, but couldn't see his own shadow. He guessed it had stayed outside, rather than venturing in here.

When he raised the torch, hundreds of eyes stared back at him. The animal Wrapped Ones were all around: on the floor, in niches cut into the walls. Some, like the sacred crocodile, had splendid coffins. Others were merely neat linen bundles with painted faces. Torchlight flickered over kneeling rams, a dainty gazelle, two stiff tubular snakes. A cat's slanted gaze reminded him of Havoc. A falcon's teardrop eyes made him think of Pirra.

The thought of them gave him courage. Come on, Hylas. Let's find the tunnel and get this over.

He found the black cat as Nebetku had described, sitting on its haunches in a niche halfway up the second tunnel on the left. It was varnished with pitch, and it stared down at him with startling yellow eyes. Behind it, the niche appeared to be backed by smooth grey stone, but this came away easily, as Nebetku had said it would.

Without giving himself time to think, Hylas jammed the Spells and the spare torch in his belt, moved the cat aside, and hoisted himself into the tunnel.

It was so narrow he couldn't wriggle in straight, but had to slant sideways with one arm stretched forwards, holding the burning torch, the other back. Mercifully, the tunnel was short. He fell out the other side on to a bumpy stone floor.

He was in a small, low chamber: rough walls hacked from the rock, then plastered over. Against them sat the red clay ancestors of Userref and Nebetku. Hylas glimpsed women in white linen dresses and scribes sitting cross-legged with scrolls and palettes in their laps. All wore dusty ropes of dried cornflowers, and had been well provided with jars of beer, water and mouldy loaves. All gazed serenely on their joyous, painted world.

The ceiling was a bright blue sky where a green

goddess watched over them with outspread arms. On one wall, painted slaves harvested wheat, and tended sleek cattle and vines with fat purple grapes, while painted ancestors feasted on wine and roast geese. Among them, a pretty girl who reminded Hylas of Meritamen ate a dish of honeycomb, while at her feet, her pet hedgehog sat tied by its leash to the leg of her chair.

The other wall was a vivid green papyrus marsh, alive with ducks and riven by blue waterways teeming with fish. Around it were date-palms and pomegranate trees, where a young man drove a chariot drawn by two prancing white horses. It reminded Hylas of the Great Green – but with no crocodiles or scorpions to hurt you. It was the Place of Reeds, where everyone was young and healthy, and there was no sickness and no pain.

All this he took in by the glimmer of his torch. Then, directly ahead, he saw the door. It was stained scarlet, to ward off demons, and it stood slightly ajar. On the walls on either side were two large black painted jackals. They lay on their bellies with their heads raised and their sharp ears pricked.

'Anpu, Lord of Silence, guards the burial chamber,' Nebetku had said. 'With my spells, He will let you pass.'

'Won't the burial chamber be sealed?' Pirra had asked.

'I left it open,' Nebetku had replied. 'Soon, I too will become a Wrapped One: *then* Rensi and Herihor can seal us in.'

Sweat trickled down Hylas' spine. Putting out his hand, he grasped the edge of the door and pulled it open.

The tunnel slanted so steeply that it was almost a shaft. Rough steps hacked from the rock led down into darkness. The silence beat at Hylas' ears: the utter silence of deep underground.

The burial chamber was smaller and plainer than the one above: no happy, painted world down here. It was crammed with dusty coffins and all that the dead would need. In the uncertain light, Hylas glimpsed stools, sandals, clothes, a board game, scrolls – Nebetku's gift to his brother? – and a bronze disc propped on a basketwork chest. He knew what that was. Last spring in the House of the Goddess, Pirra had shown him one, she'd called it a mirror. 'Bend closer and take a look,' she'd said – and giggled when he'd recoiled from the misty bronze boy within.

The air was thick with spells and the rank sweetness

of decaying lotus. Once again, he prayed that Nebetku knew what he was doing with this headband.

Suddenly, he became aware of the distant flutter of wings, as if a bird had become trapped in some forgotten tunnel of the Crocodile Tomb. And closer: faint scratchings and tiny gnat-like voices.

The hairs stood up on his forearms. The voices were coming from the far corner.

Unsteadily, he swept it with his torch. Shadows leapt, and his light flickered over rows of *shabti*, all busily weaving and sewing, kneeling at grindstones, or stirring beer. They glanced up irritably at the light. He drew back, shrouding them in darkness.

Userref's coffin lay on the ground in the middle of the chamber. It was man-shaped. The lid had feet jutting upwards and a carved and painted head: striped blue hair, serene dark-rimmed eyes, arms crossed on its chest, and below, a pair of large outstretched wings. Everything about it warned Hylas not to disturb the peace of the dead.

Except that the dead was *not* at peace. Hylas could still hear that panicky fluttering. Userref's *ba* was trapped, unable to get out.

The lid was heavier than that of the crocodile coffin, and he could only use one hand; not for all the gods of Egypt would he let go of his torch. Somehow, he managed to manoeuvre the lid till it lay aslant the coffin.

Userref's *sah* lay on its side with its neck on a limestone headrest, as if asleep. Herihor had excelled himself. The body was bandaged in intricate overlapping linen dyed red, then crisscrossed with white tapes, as if to prevent it bursting free. The breast was wreathed with crumbling poppies. The head wore a braided wig as blue as the sky, the face a mask painted green, like Userref's god Ausar, Lord of Rebirth. In front of the folded arms lay the cruel blank scroll left by Meritamen's spy – and behind, against the back, the dagger of Koronos: wound with linen spells beseeching the gods to destroy it.

They hadn't, of course. Between the bandages twisted round the dagger, Hylas caught the murderous glint of bronze.

Sweat streamed down his flanks. Userref's *sah* looked as if at any moment it might push itself up on one elbow and turn its dreadful gaze on him. 'Forgive me,' he whispered, 'for disturbing your rest.'

Wiping his hand on his thigh, Hylas bent over the coffin and reached down for the blank scroll.

The fluttering wings grew suddenly louder. Hylas felt bewilderment and pain swirling around him like dust. He spun round, his light catching the bronze mirror on the chest.

His heart jerked. The mirror threw back a cloudy image of himself – and behind it, a tall winged figure standing in the shadows.

Hylas swayed. 'Userref . . . Is that you?'

24

It stood beyond the torchlight on the other side of the coffin: a thing of dust and darkness, shifting, blurring, breaking apart.

Hylas made out a bowed head and the points of folded wings jutting above the shoulders. He felt its pain, and his dread turned to fearful pity. This had been a man. Pirra's big brother in all but name. It was Userref who had found the lion claw which had become Hylas' treasured amulet, it was Userref who had carried Havoc to safety when Thalakrea was burning. Now his spirit was in danger and needed help.

From across the dark river that flows between the living and the dead, a voice whispered in Hylas' mind, as insubstantial as mist: *Why . . .*

Hylas tightened his grip on the torch. 'N-Nebetku sends spells – to help you in the Hall of Truth . . .'

Truth . . . echoed the voice.

'I'll put them in your . . .' Wiping his free hand on his thigh, Hylas stooped over the coffin and reached for the blank scroll – *careful*, don't touch any part of the Wrapped One. He set it on the ground, then took the true scroll from his belt and held it up.

Shadowy wings rustled. The spirit's gaze chilled his skin.

The Spells for Coming Forth by Day were a tight-furled scroll, tied by tapes sealed with little clay discs. Nebetku had warned him to lay it the right way up. 'I've drawn a bee on the top end: you must put it with that end nearest the heart.'

Hylas did as he'd been told. As he set the Spells before the Wrapped One's crossed arms, a fathomless sigh breathed through his mind. *Aah* . . .

Now for the dagger of Koronos.

Again, Hylas wiped his palm on his kilt. 'He said – I could take the dagger.' But as he reached for it, an icy draught swept over him and his wrist was caught in a grip stronger than winter. He tried to draw back. He couldn't move.

Then it came to him. Userref thought Pirra was

dead. He'd sworn to keep the dagger safe, and he was guarding it still.

'She's not dead,' panted Hylas. 'Pirra's alive!'

The freezing grip only tightened.

'I can prove it! Your *wedjat* – you left it hanging on her bedpost when she was sick! I couldn't possibly know that unless she told me! She's here in Egypt, she asked me to bring it to you – she misses you so much, she wants you to be at peace!'

Peace . . . echoed the voice in his mind. The chill faded from his flesh, and he could move. But the figure loomed over the coffin, horribly close.

Hylas felt its gaze as he bent and grasped the dagger of Koronos and slid it into the empty sheath at his belt.

But when he took the *wedjat* from around his neck, the dark wings fluttered in protest, the shadowy head shook, and a finger pointed at his chest.

'You – you want me to keep the *wedjat*?' faltered Hylas.

The head bent in assent.

As Hylas slipped the thong back around his neck, he heard another sigh in his mind: not of pain, but release. *Aah* . . .

For the last time, Hylas bent over the coffin and slid the lid in place over the Wrapped One.

When he straightened up, he was alone in the burial chamber. Userref's *ba* was gone.

— ⋖—

It was much harder to breathe as he made his way back. As if a spell had been broken, he realized that he'd been down here too long. In the world of the living, surely midnight was already past.

Breathless and light-headed, he scrambled up the shaft to the ancestor chamber, then through the tunnel. Hurry, hurry.

The dagger fell to the ground with a clatter. The sheath was too loose. Hastily he dealt with that, then slid the stone slab in place to hide the tunnel, set the black cat in front and ran back to the crocodile coffin.

Where was the doorway? Nebetku had told him what to look for: a wrapped calf at a left turn, a gazelle at the next, and two paces beyond, the outer doors.

Hylas couldn't see anything resembling a calf. His mind went blank. What had he done wrong? Then he realized. He shouldn't have returned to the crocodile coffin, he should've gone the other way.

Frantically, he backtracked, stumbling past the black cat, which watched him with impassive yellow eyes. His chest was heaving. The air was thick and hot, like breathing sand.

At last the calf flickered into sight. There was the gazelle. The doors loomed out of the dark. He collapsed against them, rapping three times. 'Pirra!' he panted. 'Let me out!'

No answer.

He knocked again. Beat at the doors with his fists. They were barred from outside and didn't budge.

He waited, hearing his own laboured breaths. Beyond the doors, he caught a familiar sound, muffled by distance: Havoc's *yomp yomp* call. *Where are you?*

His torch blinked out.

He knocked again and again. 'Pirra!'

Darkness and silence.

She wasn't there.

25

Anxiously, the lion cub snuffed the wind, but she could catch no scent of the boy. All through the Light she'd waited for him in the burning land, and when the Dark had come and he still didn't appear, she'd seized her courage by the scruff and gone to find him.

As the Great Lion rose silver in the Up, she prowled the clifftop, trying to see what was happening. Many of the humans were going back across the Great Wet, howling amid an awful stink of flowers.

Suddenly, she caught muffled yowls and frantic scratching, somewhere below her. To her horror, she heard that the boy was *inside* one of the lairs of the dead humans. She called to him, trying for a good loud roar – but as always, only managing a groany yowl.

A wind that wasn't a wind stirred her scruff, and the falcon swept overhead and perched on a rock. Normally, the falcon roosted in the Dark, but now she was wide awake.

Fluffing up her neck-feathers, the falcon twisted her head right round in that way which the lion cub envied, then lifted off with a brittle alarm call: *kek-kek-kek!*

What had she seen?

The cub caught a new scent, and her hackles rose. Up from the Great Wet wafted the bitter stink of the terrible men with the flapping black hides: the men who had killed her mother and father, and nearly killed *her*. They were hunting the boy.

Tensely, the cub crept to the edge of the cliff. They were far below, coming ashore from the Great Wet. She remembered the pain in her shoulder where their flying fang had bitten deep. Her courage faltered. There were so *many* of them.

What could one small lion cub do against so many?

As the falcon rode the hot smooth Wind, the crow-men dwindled to specks, and she felt lighter and freer. The girl had been anxious, which had made the falcon anxious too – and she *hated* that. Worry was for earth-bound creatures, not falcons.

As she slid across the Sky, the falcon spotted the girl running between the huts of the humans. Something about her felt different. Yes. The girl was full of fierce, urgent purpose. This was *much* better: all falcons are fierce.

The crow-men hadn't seen the girl yet, but they would soon. The falcon knew what to do about that.

She spiralled higher towards the Moon, then tucked in her legs, folded her wings and dived. The air screamed as the earth hurtled towards her. The crow-men blundered about with their flightless wings hanging limp down their backs: so slow, so unaware. They never saw her coming because they never looked up.

At the last moment, she spread wings and tail and pulled out of the dive, shrieking. The crow-men ducked as she swept over them. They scattered, pointing at the Sky – but by then she'd left them far behind.

As she slid on to a spiral of warm air and let it carry her up the cliffs, she spotted one more. This crow-man was on his own, making for the entrance to one of the dead lairs, where a girl stood waiting: not the falcon's girl, the other one. The one *her* girl didn't like.

Silently, the falcon flew past for a closer look.

Just when Hylas was about to collapse, the doors of the Crocodile Tomb creaked open. He staggered out and fell to his knees. Couldn't see, couldn't hear; knew only the stones beneath him and the stars above and the night air pouring into his lungs.

He seemed to be lying in a small paved court cut into the cliff-face. Pirra was bending over him. He caught her spicy scent, felt her long hair tickling his cheek, and her soft hand caressing his shoulder. 'Hy-las . . .'

It wasn't her. He struggled upright. The sheath at his belt was empty. 'You – can't . . .' he gasped.

Meritamen backed into the shadows, clutching her precious bundle. 'At last I have the dagger,' she whispered. 'I'm sorry, Hy-las. But I must have it!'

'Where's Pirra?' he panted. 'What have you done with Pirra?'

'They're after you, Hy-las, they're at the foot of the cliff! Follow this path a little way down.' She pointed. 'Take that branch down there to the right, you see it? It takes you out to the desert without being seen!'

'*Where's Pirra!*'

'Remember, the right fork! Go!' With that, she vanished into the gloom.

Hylas struggled to his feet and stood swaying. He staggered a few steps. He was about to set off down the path when high overhead, Echo shrieked a warning. He spun round. He glimpsed a dark shape on the slope above the tomb. He dived sideways. Telamon's spear hissed past him and clattered on to the stones.

At the foot of the cliffs, Hylas made out Crow warriors starting up the trail. It flashed across his mind that Telamon had ordered them to wait below, while he killed the Outsider by himself. Now Telamon was leaping down into the court with his knife in his fist. They circled each other, both trying to reach Telamon's spear, lying between them on the stones. Telamon lunged for it. Hylas lashed out with his foot and caught Telamon under the chin. Telamon fell, but sprang up at once. Hylas stooped for the spear. Telamon's knife slashed the air near his face, forcing him back. Telamon snatched the spear. Again they circled. Hylas had no weapons, not even a rock. If Telamon didn't finish him off, his men would be here soon, and that would be the end.

The cliff above was too steep to climb. Hylas fled sideways, spotted what looked like a half-built tomb, made for that.

'Running away?' jeered Telamon as he scrambled after him.

The tomb was just a hole hacked from the cliff-face,

with a ledge in front and a handcart piled with rubble. No hammers or chisels, nothing he could use. Behind him Telamon moved more slowly, hampered by spear and knife. Hylas lobbed a rock at his head. Telamon dodged, lost his footing and slid, halting his fall with the butt of his spear some twenty cubits below Hylas.

The handcart's wheels were wedged with rocks. If he could keep Telamon distracted . . . 'Bad mistake leaving your men below,' he called. 'If you'd had them with you, I'd be dead by now!'

Telamon climbed towards him in silence. Moonlight gleamed on his helmet, with its rows of sliced boars' tusks. They were complete: he'd become a warrior.

'That helmet doesn't make you a man,' taunted Hylas as he prised the wedges from the wheels.

'And breaking into tombs does?' retorted Telamon.

Hylas kicked aside the last wedge and put his shoulder to the handcart. It was laden with rubble, too heavy to budge. 'Where's Pirra?' he shouted.

Telamon hesitated. 'Alive – for now. Give yourself up or she'll die!'

'Let her go! Meritamen has the dagger!'

'But I want you too,' panted Telamon. 'If you don't come down, Pirra will suffer!'

Hylas' turn to hesitate. 'I don't believe you've got her,' he said desperately.

'How would you know?' jeered Telamon.

The cart gave a jolt. It was starting to move. 'What's she wearing?' called Hylas.

Telamon didn't reply.

Hylas' mind flooded clear. 'You don't know because you haven't got her!'

No answer: he'd guessed right. With a frantic heave he sent the cart crashing over the edge.

Telamon's roar was lost in a thunder of rubble.

Hylas sped down the trail, glimpsed the fork, just as Meritamen had said. The Crow warriors were still far below; with luck, they wouldn't see where he went.

Over his shoulder, he saw Telamon lurch to his feet in clouds of dust. Hylas plunged down the right-hand fork. It was cunningly concealed, winding behind the cliffs and into a gully choked with scrub. He thought of snakes and scorpions, and muttered a quick prayer to the Lady of the Wild Things.

The cries of the Crow warriors and Telamon's roars faded behind him and still he ran, but at last he reached the bottom of the cliffs and bent double, hands on his knees.

Behind him lay the gorge that cut through the cliffs; he'd come that way the night before, when he'd slipped out to find Havoc. Ahead of him, the desert stretched flat and featureless under the Moon.

It wouldn't be long before the Crows found the gorge and came after him. *But where was Pirra?* Why hadn't she been waiting for him outside the tomb?

Suddenly, the gorge rang with hoofbeats. Then a shadowy chariot swept into view, heading straight for him.

No cover, not even a boulder. He ran, zigzagging, searching for rocks, pebbles, anything to throw.

The chariot was gaining on him, its driver bent low, the horses straining at the reins. They skittered to a halt in billows of dust and the chariot slewed round as the driver hauled on the reins.

'Jump in!' yelled Pirra. 'Hurry up, Hylas, let's *go*!'

26

'**A**re you all right?' shouted Pirra over the thundering hooves and the clatter of the chariot.

'I am now!' Hylas yelled back.

She cast him an uncertain look.

He was grinning from ear to ear, but he couldn't help it. They'd been heading west for some time, and still no sign of the Crows. Pirra flicked the reins on the horses' backs and they quickened their pace. Her dark hair streamed behind her and her small sharp face was intent. 'Where'd you learn to drive a chariot?' he cried.

'Keftiu! When my mother was away, Userref used to let me have a go in the Great Court.' She scowled. 'Why are you *grinning*? Meritamen's got the dagger – by now Telamon will have it!'

'Oh no he won't!' From his arm-sheath he whipped the dagger of Koronos and held it up.

Pirra was so astonished she nearly dropped the reins. 'How'd you manage that?'

'Luck of the gods! It didn't fit the sheath on my belt, so I swapped it with my knife! She took the wrong one!' With a whoop he waved the dagger above his head and felt its power coursing through him like fire. '*We've got it!*' he yelled. 'We can go *home*!'

The chariot lurched as the horses swerved, nearly flinging him out. 'Hold on, you idiot!' cried Pirra. 'And bend your knees!'

He shouted a laugh. 'I forgot, I've only been in a chariot once!' He went on laughing – and suddenly, Pirra was laughing too. Whooping and hooting, they went hurtling over the desert, with the dust streaming behind them and the wind blowing hot in their faces.

Echo swept down and flew alongside them, then swooped recklessly in and out between the horses' legs.

'That bird's mad!' yelled Hylas.

'Not mad.' Pirra grinned. 'Just happy that at last I can fly too!'

Behind them the sky was lightening, and above the distant grey cliffs, Hylas saw the glimmer of the star that Egyptians called Sopdet, the Flood Star. It flashed across his mind that today was the Eve of the First Drop. To him it felt like the first day ever. He had escaped the tombs and the Crows were far behind.

It felt as if he'd been reborn.

They reached a rocky outcrop where they would be out of sight of the cliffs, and Pirra hauled the chariot to a halt.

Shaking the dust from their manes, the horses threw down their heads to cough. Hylas tied them to a clump of thorn bushes, then wedged the chariot wheels with rocks to stop them running away with it, and went to check the outcrop for baboons.

Pirra climbed down on to solid earth and swayed. Her arms and shoulders ached, and she still seemed to feel the chariot jolting and twisting beneath her.

Hylas returned with a dead snake dangling from his belt. 'No baboons, and there's an overhang where we can get out of the Sun.' He blinked. 'Is that a waterskin?'

She unhitched it from the chariot and tossed it to him.

'You thought of everything,' he said admiringly.

'Except food.'

He held up the snake. 'We can't risk a fire, but it'll be all right raw.'

They gave the horses two handfuls of water each, and had one for themselves. It wasn't nearly enough, and to judge from the horses' reproachful glances, they thought so too.

In the overhang, Hylas butchered the snake and tossed the guts and head to Echo. The snake tasted better than Pirra had feared – or maybe she was just a lot hungrier than she realized – but they ate in silence.

The exhilaration had worn off. She was tired, thirsty, and beginning to wonder what they would do next. Earlier, Hylas had said they could 'go home'. But how? They had to find Havoc, and water, which meant getting back to the River without being caught. Then they had to steal a boat and travel the length of Egypt – without being caught. Then they had to persuade some ship to take two barbarians, a falcon and a lion all the way across the Sea to – where? Where was home? They couldn't return to Keftiu, and Hylas' homeland was in the grip of the Crows.

And then there was the dagger. Somehow, they had to destroy it – which meant persuading some *god* to destroy it. If they couldn't then sooner or later, the Crows would get it back.

Hylas sat against a rock with his forearms on his knees, gazing across the desert. He still wore

Nebetku's headband, and he looked very tough and self-reliant. His kilt and scarlet belt were those of an Egyptian nobleman, but with his straight Lykonian nose and long tawny warrior braids, he couldn't be anything but Akean.

He felt her watching, and gave her a lopsided smile. She was suddenly acutely aware of her dishevelled appearance, and how beautiful Meritamen must have looked by moonlight. Crossly, she started undoing her braids and ripping out the flowers and feathers.

Hylas, too, began unravelling his hair. 'Why did she let me out, instead of you?'

Pirra told him how Meritamen had stopped her before she'd reached the tomb, and had threatened to leave him there to die unless Pirra let the Egyptian girl take her place. 'I couldn't see how else to save you, but I only said yes if she'd set me free. While Herihor took her to the tomb, Rensi and I ran down to the stables. No one was guarding them, they were all up at the tombs. I was going to steal a chariot, to help us escape, but I didn't know if you were still alive.' She frowned. 'I saw the Crows coming up from the River. I was getting desperate, but then Herihor came running. He said Meritamen had let you out and taken the dagger, *and* shown you a way down to the desert. They helped me steal a chariot. The rest you know.'

She watched Echo hold down the snake's head with one foot, and shred it with her beak. 'That girl never told me the Crows were already on the West Bank,' she added bitterly.

'I don't think she knew,' said Hylas.

'You're not trying to *defend* her?'

'Well she did show me that trail, she didn't have to do that.'

She snorted. 'Would you defend her if she was ugly?'

'Pirra. You don't need to worry about Meritamen.'

Heat stole into her face, and she briskly combed her hair with her fingers, then drew her knife and started cutting off her dress below the knee. It would make walking easier, and they could use the remnants to bind their heads against the Sun.

After that, she unwound Nebetku's spells from the dagger of Koronos. Then Hylas polished the blade with sand till it shone. 'Strange how it worked out,' he said thoughtfully. 'Telamon wanted to have the glory of killing me all by himself, so he left his men and went on ahead. If he'd been less proud, he'd have had that tomb surrounded and I'd be dead.'

'Don't even say such things!' said Pirra.

There was silence between them. In a low voice, she asked what had happened in the tomb.

Haltingly, he told her: about being trapped in the coffin and the *medu netjer* coming alive, and the tunnel and the *shabti* – and finally, the winged figure in the burial chamber.

It was even worse than she'd imagined.

'But it's all right,' he said. 'After I'd swapped the scrolls, he wasn't there any more, which must mean he's free – or at least, on his way.'

For the first time, Pirra noticed that on his chest, he wore *two* amulets: his own lion claw, and Userref's *wedjat*. 'You've still got it.'

'I tried to give it to him, but he wanted me to keep it.'

'Why?'

'I don't know. Here. Take it.'

'– No,' she said slowly. 'Keep it. He wants you to have it. He must have a reason.' Suddenly, her spirits plummeted. They might have the dagger of Koronos, but Userref was still dead, and nothing would ever bring him back. And even if she and Hylas did find a way to leave Egypt, they would also be leaving Telamon and Alekto unpunished – and Userref unavenged.

On her rock, Echo sicked up a neat pellet of snake-bones and glittery scales. Hylas went to the edge of the overhang and stood looking out. The Sun beat fiercely, and the desert shimmered in the heat. He picked up the waterskin and hefted it. 'Not enough for a day, not with two people and two horses.' He looked at her. Then he said what she was thinking. 'We've got to go back to the River.'

'I know. But they'll be watching the gorge.'

'Oh, yes.'

'Did you see any other way through the cliffs?'

'I think there's a sort of dip, like a saddle, to the south. We might be able to climb it and get across that way.'

'If they're not watching that too.'

'Yes, but what choice do we have?'

Again Pirra felt the dread in her stomach. Fate, the gods, Havoc, the need for water – all tightening around them like a net. 'There's nothing for it,' she said. 'We've got to go back.'

The day had crawled by in a daze of heat, and as dusk fell, they set off.

The plan was to leave the horses to make their own way through the gorge, thus distracting the Crows, while Hylas and Pirra climbed the saddle to the south. It wasn't much of a plan, but it was the best they could do.

They approached the gorge in a wide loop, then slowed to a walk. The horses smelt the River and lifted their heads. Silently, Hylas unhitched them and led them to the mouth of the gorge. All was quiet; no sign of Crows. As soon as he released them, the horses flicked up their tails and trotted off towards the River.

Hylas glanced at Pirra. She'd rubbed her white dress with dust, so that it wouldn't show up in the dark, and he'd done the same with his kilt. In the gloom, she looked pale and resolute.

To his relief, they found a goat trail almost at once: steep, but not impossible. As they climbed, he prayed that Havoc would catch their scent and find them on the other side.

After a while, the path levelled off and the wind strengthened. They'd reached the top. The Moon hadn't yet risen, but by starlight Hylas saw the dark workshops and villages far to the north. Below him a shadowy field, then the silver glitter of the River. On the bank, he made out a large boat with a splendid canopy: he guessed that belonged to Meritamen. Further north, moored just off a wooded islet, the dark bulk of the Crows' ship.

Pirra touched his arm and pointed. The horses were cantering out of the gorge, followed by several Crow warriors. Pirra's grin showed white in the gloom. Hylas nodded. So far, so good. With luck, the warriors wouldn't be able to see that the horses were riderless, and they'd go after them, thinking they were chasing their quarry.

The saddle was steeper going down, but thornscrub gave some cover, and at the bottom they found themselves among tumbled boulders.

Forty paces ahead, reeds hid the River from view. Hylas' heart leapt. Among the reeds lay something he hadn't spotted from the saddle: a small rowing boat drawn up on the bank.

'We're in luck!' breathed Pirra, running forwards.

Hylas started after her. Then he glimpsed Havoc crouching among the reeds. Her ears were pricked, her silver eyes staring past him at something he couldn't see.

'Pirra!' he whispered.

At that moment, Havoc fled, and Crow warriors rose up from the shadows and surrounded Pirra. '*Run!*' she screamed.

The lion cub fled through the reeds with the girl's screams clawing at her ears. But how could the cub help, against so many crow-men?

Even the boy had run away, he also knew it was hopeless. The cub smelt him hiding in the boulders at the bottom of the slope.

But what was he doing now? One of the horses had drunk its fill and was wandering past, snorting and tossing its head. The boy was creeping towards it. He was moving as quietly as he could – which wasn't very quiet – but not hunting, he was *letting* the horse see him. Gently, he scratched its neck. Then he did something astonishing: *he scrambled on to its back.*

Ah, this was clever. He and the horse were galloping

towards the gorge. But they hadn't seen the other crow-men, lots of them, lying in wait at the mouth of the gorge.

The lion cub didn't hesitate. Bursting from the reeds, she went racing to his rescue, dodging between the little mud dens of the humans. A dog flew at her. She swatted it aside with one paw and it hit a wall and ran away, whimpering. Three more leapt after her, barking savagely. She spun round, snarling and slashing with her claws. To her surprise, all three turned tail and fled for the nearest den.

She sped towards the gorge. The boy and the horse were nearing the trap, where many crow-men waited behind their boulders. They didn't see the cub. Seizing her courage in her jaws, she sprang, lashing out with ferocious snarls that were very nearly roars. The crow-men scattered like frightened mice, and the horse *finally* caught the cub's scent and thundered up the gorge, still with the boy clinging to its back.

Good. For now, he was safe. Feeling better than she had in a long time, the lion cub bounded to the top of the cliffs.

A hot wind was blowing from the burning lands where the boy had gone. He would return when he could, and come for her, and together they would find some way to rescue the girl from the crow-men. The cub knew this because she knew that she and the boy and girl were of the same pride, and they belonged together.

If only the falcon was as certain of that as the cub.

Wistfully, the lion cub raised her muzzle to the Dark, but she heard no familiar hiss of wings, and no exasperating yet oddly comforting bird glided in to perch nearby.

The falcon had found a beautiful ant-free roost in a tree overlooking the reeds. It was perfect.

Everything about this place was perfect, and made for falcons: trees for roosting, wet for bathing, breeze to cool your underwings and snatch the heat from your beak, and reeds full of delicious slow waterbirds and crunchy damselflies. There were even other falcons on the crags; not too many, just enough to make it interesting.

And yet – she was on her own. No boy, no lion cub. Most importantly, no girl.

The falcon barely remembered the Egg. Her real Beginning had been meeting the girl. That strange featherless face. No beak, just a soft little nose . . . But the girl's eyes were large and dark as a falcon's, and she had a falcon's fierce spirit and longing to fly.

The falcon *missed* her. Yes, even now in this perfect

place. And she sensed that the girl was in trouble, she could feel her struggling to be free. The falcon felt a horrible breathless panic, as if she too was trapped and unable to fly.

She couldn't settle to roost. She didn't know what to do.

The lion cub was *thirsty*, so while the crow-men yowled angrily at each other and at the girl, and the Great Lion rose silver in the Up, she found another way down to a place by the Great Wet that was free of humans and dogs.

Warily, she snuffed the mud. Giant lizards *had* been here, but weren't here now, so she padded to the edge and hunkered down to drink.

She leapt back in alarm. *There was a she-lion in the wet.*

The lion cub waited. The she-lion didn't come out. The lion cub belly-crawled closer.

There it was again, staring up at her. Not unfriendly, just startled and curious, a bit like her.

The lion cub extended a cautious forepaw.

So did the she-lion.

Both patted the wet at the *exact same moment*, then withdrew.

The lion cub had an astonishing idea. Pouncing on

the wet, she stomped all over the she-lion – who disappeared. Backing away, the cub waited. Gradually, the wet stopped shivering, and the she-lion reappeared.

The lion cub's idea had been right. She sat down, struggling to take it in. *That she-lion in the wet was herself.* No wonder those dogs had been scared of her. She wasn't a cub any more – she was a huge, powerful, *grown-up* lioness.

28

A leader feels no fear and no doubt, Telamon told himself as he strode along the river-bank. A leader turns every setback into victory.

But inside he was seething. All day he and his men had lain in wait for Hylas, knowing he had to return to the West Bank. As night fell, they'd redoubled their vigilance: he was bound to sneak in under cover of darkness.

And now this. Ilarkos, his second-in-command, had just run up out of the gloom. 'He got away, my lord,' he panted.

'How?' Telamon said icily.

'He caught one of the horses and made it through the gorge –'

'– the gorge which you were guarding.'

'He was too fast, and the men – they saw something.'

'*What?*'

'A – a great lion . . . or a demon in the body of a lion.'

Telamon stared at him. 'You mean they were *frightened*?'

Ilarkos hung his head.

So that's another bad choice I've made, thought Telamon: sending half the men to the gorge and the rest along the bank, with me in the middle watching it all go wrong.

And no help from those filthy Egyptians. The men guarding the tombs had stayed stubbornly at their post, and Meritamen's slaves had remained by their boat, while in the villages and workshops, all was dark and silent, everyone waiting for the barbarians to leave.

Telamon's spirits plummeted. Every choice he'd made had turned to disaster. If he'd kept a close watch on Meritamen, he would be holding the dagger in his fist. If he'd taken his men with him to that tomb, Hylas would be dead. He thought how Alekto would sneer when she found out, and how she would enjoy telling Koronos when they were back in Mycenae.

At least you've got Pirra, he told himself. Yes. Make the most of that.

Meritamen hurried towards him, twisting her hands. She'd done that earlier when he'd found her among the tombs, soon after Hylas escaped. 'I have your precious dagger,' she'd said with contempt. Contempt which had turned to horror when Telamon had uncovered not the dagger of Koronos, but a battered old knife.

Now it was Telamon's turn to regard *her* with contempt. Why hadn't she fled back to Pa-Sobek? Hadn't she done enough?

'Don't hurt the girl,' she pleaded. 'She hasn't done anything wrong!'

'What do you care?' he snarled.

'I've done enough harm! I can't have her blood on my hands!'

Telamon strode past her without a word.

Pirra was dwarfed by the warriors who'd caught her. It hadn't been necessary to tie her arms behind her back, but they'd done it anyway, and this pleased Telamon a lot. Pirra had always regarded him as a barbarian. The last time he'd confronted her, on Keftiu, she'd told him that Hylas was all that was best in Akea, while he was all that was worst.

Well, that was about to change.

She stood very straight, staring past him as if he didn't exist. Her face was smooth as a mask beneath its Egyptian paint, but she was afraid, he could tell.

He made a show of twisting the little amethyst falcon on his wrist that had once been hers. He put his hands on his hips and let her see his belt, with its plaques of Keftian gold. They had been hers, too.

Her stare never wavered.

Strange. Meritamen was prettier, but Pirra burned with a fire that drew you in and didn't let go.

At his elbow, Meritamen said: 'I must return to Pa-Sobek. I can take her with me. Please, she is no use to you!'

'I wouldn't be too sure of that,' he said pleasantly. Then to Pirra: 'It seems Hylas has fled. *Fled*,' he repeated. 'Scrambled on to a horse and *fled* to the desert.'

'Good,' she said, still without looking at him.

He smiled. 'He left you without a second thought. Not so brave now, is he?'

'He was outnumbered twenty to one; I told him to go – it would've been madness to fight.'

Telamon was about to reply when it came to him that he could use her as bait. He turned to Meritamen. 'I'll take you across the River to Pa-Sobek, but your crew stays here, I want my own men at the oars.' Then to Ilarkos: 'Pick four men to row the boat and take the rest to the ship and make ready to leave. I'll return directly with the Lady Alekto. Then we're starting for home.'

Murmurs of relief from the men, and Ilarkos' face cleared. 'What about the Keftian girl, my lord?'

'She comes with me,' said Telamon. 'I want the Outsider to see her.'

Ilarkos looked puzzled. 'But he's out in the desert.'

'Oh, he'll come back,' said Telamon. 'He won't leave her. He'll come back and he'll see her – with the Lady Alekto.'

Ilarkos swallowed. Meritamen's hands tightened.

Pirra tried not to flinch. 'Using me as bait won't work. Hylas isn't mad enough to try and rescue me.' But Telamon could see that she wasn't so sure. And she was frightened of Alekto. Everyone was frightened of Alekto.

Except me, he thought. Alekto is only a woman. She doesn't matter.

How could he have doubted that the gods were on his side? Everything was working out as if he'd planned it. Earlier, he'd agreed with Alekto that she would be waiting on the quay at dawn; he'd told her that by then it would all be over and they could head for home, because by then he would have the dagger of Koronos and the still-warm heart of the Outsider. Well, he didn't, not yet. But instead, he would give her Pirra – and Alekto would make Pirra give them the dagger *and* Hylas.

Once again, Telamon was glad that his grandfather had sent Alekto with him to Egypt, because now he could make use of her talents. He suspected that he could never bring himself to hurt Pirra – but Alekto would positively enjoy it.

For a moment, his spirit quailed at the thought. Then he remembered Koronos. Be a man, he told himself. It's what Koronos would do.

'Hylas won't come,' repeated Pirra – as if saying it could make it true.

'Yes he will,' said Telamon. 'When he hears you scream.'

Dawn on the Day of the First Drop. A sky like beaten copper and a hot wind blowing from the desert. On the East Bank, all Pa-Sobek was gathered above the stone steps, waiting for the priests to declare that the River was beginning to rise.

Nobody cared about the Hati-aa's boat, which had docked on the quay to let the Lady Meritamen disembark, and the beautiful stranger go aboard. Let the barbarians return to their own land. Soon Iteru would rise and Egypt would be reborn from its waters, as it had been reborn every year since the Beginning.

Huddled beneath the canopy on the Hati-aa's boat, Pirra could already feel the River waking up. It didn't care about her. No one did. Even Meritamen, who'd tried to defend her, had fled. The Crow warriors at the oars averted their eyes, as if she was already dead, and behind her, Telamon stood with his hand on the steering-paddle, gazing over her head. He had handed her over to Alekto.

Alekto sat a little apart from her on the bench beneath the canopy. The wind moulded her silken robes to her graceful limbs, and tendrils of dark hair caressed her lovely throat. Since coming aboard, she hadn't glanced at Pirra, but now she turned and regarded her coolly, as if she was some doomed creature caught in a snare.

I will not scream, Pirra told herself.

But she knew that when the time came, she would. And yet she wasn't conscious of being afraid. She felt the pain in her elbows and wrists and the trapped feeling of her arms being tied behind her. And she felt a vast disbelief: this wasn't happening, it wasn't real. What was real was Havoc prowling the cliffs, and Echo waking up in some tree and tidying her feathers – and Hylas . . .

'Who gave you the scar?' said Alekto, startling her.

'I did,' said Pirra.

'How?'

'– The tip of a burning stick.'

The beautiful lips drew back in a strange half-grimace, half-smile. 'That would have hurt.'

'Yes,' said Pirra.

'Ah.'

Turning her head, Pirra stared into the murky green water. If she leapt overboard, she would drown. But she couldn't even escape that way because of the two Crow warriors who sat at the oars beside her. The one nearest was young, about Hylas' age, his chin dotted with pimples and the beginnings of a beard. Pirra smelt his rawhide armour and oniony sweat. He felt her glance and scowled. No help there.

'Your slave bled a lot,' Alekto said dreamily.

Pirra stiffened.

'We thought when he jumped in the River that crocodiles would be drawn by the smell. Instead, he spoilt our fun and drowned. Still. They say that drowning is one of the most painful ways to die.'

Pirra clenched her fists behind her back. Whatever happens to me, she told Alekto silently, you will pay for that.

Very deliberately, she let her gaze fall to the little

pouch at her belt that contained the spell Nebetku had helped her make.

'What is that you have there?' said Alekto in a soft voice.

Pirra pretended to give a guilty start. 'Please, it's n-nothing,' she stammered, feigning terror, which wasn't hard.

Alekto's beautiful lips curled. 'Something precious, from your fair-haired Outsider?'

'No!' protested Pirra. 'Just an amulet, to protect me from drowning!'

Alekto signed to the young warrior, who cut the pouch from Pirra's belt and handed it to Alekto. 'Oh you won't drown,' she said as she weighed it in her palm. She seemed about to toss it overboard; then on impulse, she tied it to her own belt.

Pirra bent her head as if dejected, hiding the hot surge of hatred coursing through her. Whatever happens to me, she begged the Goddess silently, heed my spell. Make this woman pay for what she did to Userref.

And then, because she was in Egypt, she prayed to the goddess Het-Heru, who most resembled her own Keftian Goddess, and finally, because she was desperate, she prayed to Hylas' Lykonian goddess, the Lady of the Wild Things.

The water in midstream was getting choppy, and the boat lurched. The oarsmen grunted, struggling to hold her steady. Distractedly, Pirra noticed that they were taking the wrong route: the shorter, more dangerous one.

Over on the West Bank, she saw smoke rising from the cooking-fires of Gesa and Tjebu, and people moving about, beginning their day. Straight ahead, she saw the rocky saddle which she and Hylas had climbed only a short while ago. Below it on the bank, date-palms waved in the wind, and closer still, the Crows' black ship rocked near the tip of the little wooded island. Pirra saw warriors on board, letting down the oars and making ready to leave.

The thought of Hylas was like a knife twisting in her chest. Stay away, stay alive, she told him. *Don't* try to rescue me, that's what they want.

A swampy smell of River brought her back. Glancing down, she saw a small puddle of water beneath her feet. It was barely enough to wet her toes, but it hadn't been there before.

She remembered that lurch in midstream. Had they struck a submerged log, or a rock? Had the River tired of these barbarians? Or was the spell which now hung from Alekto's belt already beginning to work? Was it going to sink the boat?

Alekto hadn't noticed the water. It hadn't yet touched her smooth hennaed feet in their gilded sandals.

Suddenly, among the date-palms on the bank, Pirra glimpsed a flash of fair hair ducking behind a tree-trunk. Oh no Hylas, no. Swiftly she turned her head, praying that Alekto hadn't seen.

That prayer went unanswered. Alekto leant forwards and called eagerly to Telamon. 'Over there!'

29

irra saw Hylas duck out of sight among the date-palms. Behind him lay open ground: if he fled that way, the warriors on the Crow ship would shoot him down. But a belt of reeds fringed the bank near his hiding place, he could still escape into that.

Alekto had seen this too. 'Order the ship to cross to the bank and finish him off,' she told Telamon. 'If he gets into those reeds, we've lost him.'

'*I* give the orders!' snarled Telamon.

Again the boat lurched, pitching Pirra forwards. The swampy smell was stronger, water was sloshing around her ankles. She felt oddly calm, as if she wasn't here in the boat, but a falcon soaring overhead, gazing down at the tiny humans. 'What do you do now,

266

Telamon?' she called over her shoulder. 'We're sinking. If you send your ship after Hylas, what happens to us?'

Telamon glared down at her, but she could see the doubt in his eyes.

Beside her, Alekto flicked her a curious glance, which Pirra ignored. If Hylas was to have a chance of escape, she had to keep them distracted. 'We're sinking,' she repeated. 'If you don't order your ship to come and rescue us, we're all going to drown!'

'No we're not,' he muttered. At the top of his voice, he yelled an order to his second-in-command on the ship: 'Ilarkos, stay where you are but get the men to the oars and make ready to cast us a rope!' To the four warriors in the boat: 'Row faster, we can do it!'

But the young warrior near Pirra was frightened, the lump in his throat jerking up and down as he cast about for something to scoop out the water. There was nothing; the Egyptian crew, angered at being ordered off their craft, had taken their pails with them.

'You'll have to use your hands,' Pirra told him mockingly.

'Shut up, Pirra,' growled Telamon.

And still Hylas hadn't moved from the date-palms. Why didn't he run for the reeds while he had the chance? He couldn't help her now, no one could.

Raising her voice so that everyone could hear, she spoke to the young warrior. 'You took the wrong route over the River! This is the shortest way, but it's also the most dangerous, that's why Egyptians avoid it!' She forced a laugh. 'The River doesn't want us, we're all going to drown!'

'Row harder!' Telamon barked at the oarsmen. 'Not far now!'

Muddy water was slapping their ankles. Alekto's lips tightened with disgust as she twitched the hem of her robes clear. Pirra noticed that henna from her feet was tingeing the water red.

Suddenly, the lead oarsmen cried out in alarm.

Pirra's belly turned over. Not far from them on a sandbank, crocodiles were snaking down to the water, slipping under the surface. She thought of her spell, tied to Alekto's belt. It was working in ways more terrible than she'd imagined.

The young warrior was panicking and bailing frantically with his hands. The lead oarsmen were doing the same.

'Keep rowing, you fools!' hissed Alekto. Her face was taut and she was gripping one of the poles that supported the canopy.

'It doesn't matter what they do,' Pirra told her. 'Either we drown, or the crocodiles get us.'

'No one's going to die,' snapped Telamon. 'We're nearly at the ship and they've got the rope to haul us in!'

Ilarkos was leaning over the ship's side, and now he cast them the rope. In the boat, the lead oarsman caught it and a cheer went up. The boat gave another lurch, but this time it was the men on the ship, hauling them in.

Telamon barked a laugh. 'Told you, Pirra, we're saved!'

Luckily, the Egyptian crew hadn't taken their landing-plank with them, and now two oarsmen extended it towards the ship, where men reached down and grabbed its free end. The boat was pitching and rolling, the landing-plank wouldn't stay in place for long. The oarsmen in front realized this and scrambled up it to safety.

'Cowards!' snarled Telamon. But he was already pushing past Alekto, grabbing Pirra and staggering up the plank. Pirra glimpsed swirling water, then the two remaining oarsmen scrambling after her. She heard a splash as the plank fell in the River and was swept away.

Then Telamon pulled her onto the ship.

At that moment, a scream rang out: a scream of such inhuman terror as Telamon had never heard in his life.

He turned – everyone turned – and there in midstream was the fast-sinking prow of the Hati-aa's boat, and clinging to it, her yellow robes floating, was Alekto, screaming at the crocodiles converging on her like the rays of some evil green star.

'To the oars!' bellowed Ilarkos. 'We can reach her in time!'

Telamon's mind raced. You must be strong, he told himself. This is the will of the gods. 'No!' he shouted to Ilarkos. 'We stay where we are!'

Ilarkos was aghast. 'But, my lord . . .'

Telamon glanced over his shoulder, and for an instant his eyes met Alekto's. You must be strong, he told himself again.

Clenching his teeth, he made himself turn his back on his kinswoman. He heard crashing water and terrible bubbling screams: muffled, then shockingly loud – then abruptly cut off.

He looked back. She was gone. Nothing left but crimson water. He breathed out. The gods *meant* this to happen. It was Alekto's destiny to die, so that he might triumph.

And now it was his destiny to kill the Outsider.

Telamon dragged Pirra across to the other side of the boat, the side facing the West Bank, and shoved her in front of him, in full view of the date-palms where Hylas was hiding. She was sick with horror, Alekto's gurgling cries still ringing in her ears. She could hardly summon the will to struggle.

'Look what I've got, Hylas!' Telamon roared over her head, twisting her arms higher behind her back. It was agonizing, but she bit back a scream, knowing that would draw Hylas into the open, into arrowshot.

Telamon was horribly strong, holding her with one muscled forearm across her chest. She tried to bite, but couldn't reach. He clamped tighter, his fingers digging into her upper arm. He was enjoying this.

A shadow slid across the ship. Telamon shouted a command to an archer beside him, who raised his bow and aimed at the sky. In horror, Pirra saw Echo wheeling overhead. 'No!' she screamed.

The arrow flew wide, and Echo slid unharmed across the Sun.

'Hear that, Hylas?' Telamon was grinning, Pirra could hear it in his voice.

'Don't hurt her!' yelled Hylas from the trees. 'Take the dagger! I'll throw it over to you – but first let her go free!'

Telamon's laugh was loud in her ears. 'No, I'll have the dagger first – *then* you get the girl!'

Silence from the date-palms.

'Hylas, I mean it!' called Telamon. With his free hand, he jabbed the point of his knife under Pirra's chin. 'Throw me the dagger! Only when I've got it will I give you the girl!'

The dagger of Koronos flew through the air and thudded on to the deck at Telamon's feet.

Flinging Pirra to Ilarkos, he snatched it up. Its smooth hilt fitted his fist like part of his own flesh, and as he held it high, its blade flashed in the Sun and turned to flame. He felt its power coursing through his veins, and his heart swelled with painful pride. 'I am Telamon of the House of Koronos,' he roared, 'and I have regained the dagger of my Ancestors!' His voice rang clear across the River, telling them all – the doubters, the sneerers, anyone who'd ever questioned his right to lead – that the gods had chosen *him* to be leader of his clan.

'We had a bargain – let Pirra go!' shouted Hylas, his voice cutting through Telamon's dreams.

Telamon ignored him, turning the dagger this way and that, admiring its strong straight spine and the lethal sweep of its blade.

'You have a raft on board,' called Hylas. 'Send two of your men with the girl! Bring her to the bank!'

Telamon glanced from the date-palms to Pirra. 'No,' he cried.

Pirra spat in his face. 'So much for the honour of the House of Koronos,' she sneered.

Slowly, Telamon wiped her spit from his cheek. Coldly, he ordered Ilarkos to hold her close to the edge: 'I want the Outsider to see her. Good. Now put your knife to her throat.' Then, with the steady hands of a leader, he took his bow from a slave and readied an arrow.

'Outsider!' he called, and his voice was as strong and sure as bronze: as strong and sure as Koronos himself. 'Stop skulking behind those trees and show yourself!'

'No, Hylas, no!' screamed Pirra. 'He has a bow, he'll kill you!'

Telamon laughed. 'For once she's right, Hylas, I will! But if you don't step out into the open, you'll have to watch her die first!'

30

'Out in the open, Hylas!' shouted Telamon. 'Or I will kill her!'

The ship lay just off the island and well within arrowshot of where Hylas hid behind the palms. He saw Telamon standing on board with an arrow nocked to his bow, and beside him, the warrior named Ilarkos, holding Pirra: one burly forearm clamped across her, the other with a knife to her throat. Ilarkos had a weatherbeaten face and the steady eyes of a man trained to obey. He wouldn't hesitate to kill her.

'Hylas, don't!' screamed Pirra, struggling in his grip.

'One word,' yelled Telamon. 'All I have to do is give the word, and he'll slit her throat!'

Telamon meant it, Hylas could see that. His eyes were wild: nothing left of the boy who'd been his friend, all that scorched away by his hunger for power, and by the final step he'd just taken, leaving his own kin to die. The churning red horror in midstream was stamped on Hylas' mind: a white arm flung up, reaching for the sky, then dragged under for ever.

'I will do it, Hylas! Do you want to watch Pirra die?'

It came to Hylas that even if he slunk off now and made his way back to Akea – even if he found Issi and they created a home together far from the Crows – it would never be any good, because he wouldn't be with Pirra.

All this flashed through his mind in a heartbeat.

Then he stepped out into the open and Telamon shot him in the chest.

Hylas lay on his back, squinting up at palm fronds slashing the Sun to ribbons. He heard Pirra screaming his name. He wasn't dead.

His head ached. He was going to have a vision. It hurt to breathe, he felt as if someone had kicked him in the chest. With his free hand he felt his breastbone, where Telamon had shot him. No blood. His fingers found the heavy bronze *wedjat*.

The wedjat . . . He saw the dent where Telamon's arrow had struck it and bounced off.

Pirra was still screaming his name: '*Hylas, get under cover!*'

Telamon's arrow lay beside him, the tip of its obsidian head snapped off. He grabbed it, struggled to his feet and swayed. Time stretched. Then the veils shrouding the spirit world blew apart – and he *saw*.

Out in the River, the swirling water became a vast green crocodile lashing its tail. Behind him, the desert wind blew a great twisting column of sand that coalesced into a towering woman with the head of a lion and red hair of streaming dust. Above him, vast wings spread across the sky, then drew together and became a dark bolt hurtling out of the Sun . . .

'*Hylas, get under cover!*' screamed Pirra again.

Her voice cut through the vision, and time snapped back.

On the ship, Telamon was taking aim at him again.

Hylas leapt sideways. The dark bolt struck. Telamon staggered, bellowing with rage, his bow falling over the side, blood pouring from a wound in his forehead. Echo swept off with a scornful cry.

Ilarkos must have loosened his grip on Pirra to help

him, because she seized her chance and leapt overboard.

'*Pirra!*' yelled Hylas.

But the water closed over her head and she was gone.

Murky water filling eyes and mouth, a booming in her ears. The water was so muddy she couldn't tell up from down, and with her arms tied behind her, all she could do was kick.

Don't splash, she thought, you'll draw the crocodiles. Her mind shied away from the horror in midstream. How long before they finished Alekto and came for her?

Her chest was bursting, she *had* to have air. Her foot struck mud. She floundered, mud sucking her feet. She kicked as hard as she could – and exploded from the water.

Gasping and spluttering, she caught a choppy vision of reeds, but couldn't see Hylas. Behind her on the ship, the Crows were no longer shooting at the shore, they were manning the oars and rowing away.

Then she saw why. Dark figures were racing down from the saddle, shooting at the Crows: bowmen with black skin as dark as Kem's. It *was* Kem, there he was among the others, raining down arrows on the Crows.

They're going to hit me, she thought. A bubble of shocked laughter rose in her throat. What if she survived Telamon and the crocodiles, only to be cut down by a friend?

Arrows hissed over her head as she struggled towards the shore, while Telamon yelled at his men to row, row.

Her ears were still booming. She saw the Hati-aa's men streaming down from the Houses of Eternity, and Kem and his bowmen vanishing over the saddle. She saw Telamon raise the dagger of Koronos in triumph as his black ship glided off downriver, its prow slicing through the waters stained red with his kinswoman's blood.

And suddenly there was Hylas, alive, wading towards her, and pulling her into his arms. They were both soaking wet, laughing and crying, and he was clutching her so tightly she could hardly breathe.

'But he *shot* you,' she panted, 'I saw him do it!'

'The *wedjat* saved me.'

'The *wedjat* . . .' Over her shoulder, she saw the red water and the flick of a scaly green tail. 'That was why Userref wanted you to have it,' she faltered. 'He saved you. And now I have avenged his death.'

Hylas wasn't listening, he was clumsily cutting her bonds with Telamon's arrowhead, muttering something she couldn't hear and passing his hands over her arms and face, as if making sure that she was truly alive.

Neither of them saw the crocodile. It's always the one you don't see that gets you.

But in that frozen moment as they stood together in the shallows and the giant lizard burst out at them, something sprang at it from the bank. Pirra saw a great golden blur leaping right over her head as Havoc launched her attack. Then lion and crocodile were locked in combat, rolling, thrashing, the crocodile twisting round to snap, Havoc hanging on with her claws and clamping her fangs into its throat.

The crocodile was huge, yet Havoc was stronger: a cub no longer, but a full-grown lioness – and finally, she *knew* it. Still with her jaws clamped on the monster's throat, she reared out of the water, gave one tremendous shake from side to side that snapped its spine, and flung its lifeless body in the mud. Then she swung round to face Hylas and Pirra, her muzzle red with blood and her golden eyes ablaze – and *roared* her triumph to the sky.

A little later, the Hati-aa's men found them, and

stood in awe before these two barbarians whom the great gods of Egypt, Heru and Sekhmet, had protected with their sacred creatures: the dark-eyed girl with a falcon on her shoulder, and the boy with hair the colour of the Sun and a huge lioness standing guard at his side.

31

The black bowmen had vanished into the desert, the Hati-aa's men had returned to Pa-Sobek, and the West Bank was at peace.

Rensi took Hylas and Pirra to Nebetku's workshop, where Hylas told the dying man how he'd put the Spells for Coming Forth by Day in Userref's coffin. To prove it, he described what the Wrapped One had looked like, which finally reassured Nebetku that the barbarian had kept his word.

After that, Berenib made Hylas and Pirra wash, then fed them a huge meal of bean porridge, date cakes and pomegranate wine, and they curled up and slept for the rest of the day.

Hylas woke around midnight. Pirra was still

whiffling quietly, but he knew he wouldn't sleep any more, so he set off for the desert to find Havoc.

The elation of survival had worn off, and as he picked his way through the gorge, he felt shaken and low. He kept seeing Telamon brandishing the dagger of Koronos, and that churning horror in midstream. The Crows had the dagger. And here he was, far from Akea, with everything to do again.

But what really haunted him was the vision. It had been stronger and clearer than any he'd ever had before – and it had kept him transfixed and out in the open, for Telamon to shoot at. What if next time he had a vision, it wasn't himself he put in danger, but Havoc? Or Pirra?

In the end, he didn't find Havoc, *she* found *him*, emerging silently from the dark, as lions do. She leapt at him and put her huge forepaws on his shoulders, rubbing her furry cheek against his and telling him in groany lion-talk about her successful hunt. This made him feel a bit better. And he was pleased that she'd finally realized that she was no longer a cub, but a powerful lioness.

Suddenly, Havoc gave an eager *whuff* and bounded off into the gloom. Someone yelped, and Hylas made out a shadowy figure trying to stand in the face of the lioness's determined welcome.

Kem pushed her off, grinning from ear to ear.

'The bowmen on the ridge,' said Hylas. 'Pirra said she saw you among them.'

Kem's grin widened. His short hair was caked in red ochre, and the scars on his cheeks had been picked out in yellow. Over his shoulder was a longbow, with a spare bowstring wound around his temples. In his fist he held an Egyptian warrior's crescent-moon axe.

'No one will ever call you a coward now, my friend,' said Hylas, eyeing the axe.

Kem laughed. 'I took it from the stables. The guards, they all up on the hill watching the tombs.' He paused. 'After we seen off the Crows, we had to run away quick time. Didn't want the Hati-aa's men to spot us.'

'You were there when we needed you. Thanks.'

Kem brushed that aside.

'But why come so far into Egypt?' said Hylas. 'You could've found a patrol right on the border, much nearer your own country. It would've been less risky.'

Kem shrugged. 'Thought you might need help. And I had a debt to pay.'

'And you've repaid it. That reminds me. Pirra sends her thanks. She said she's sorry she ever doubted you.'

Kem looked pleased. 'You got a brave girl there,' he said, digging at the sand with his heel. 'Not many like her. In my country she'd be worth many cows.'

'Shall I tell her that?'

Another laugh. 'Better not!'

On impulse, Hylas took off his lion-claw amulet and held it out. 'Here. For you.'

Kem was delighted. 'This the *best* thing! You know what is my real name?' He made a clicking sound. 'That means "lion"!'

'Ah, that's good,' smiled Hylas.

Kem glanced over his shoulder to where several tall young black men were squatting in the gloom, staring at Hylas and Havoc with awe. 'We got canoes hidden. Long way back. Nobody knows we're here, not even my father.'

'So you found him all right.'

Kem nodded proudly, and Hylas felt a flash of envy, and the familiar shame that came over him whenever he thought of his own father, whom he'd never known, and who had died a coward.

'Hylas,' said Kem. 'The years I was gone, my father never gave up hope. Your sister – don't you give up hope.'

Hylas didn't reply. Havoc leant against him, and he raked his fingers through her deep coarse fur. The Crows had the dagger, and he was far from Akea, at the very edge of the world. He was sick of living on hope.

The Moon had set by the time he found his way back to the West Bank. He expected the settlements to be asleep, but instead he found mourners rocking and wailing outside Nebetku's workshop, and Rensi and Herihor standing together, crying.

'He died a little while ago,' said Pirra, 'but I won't grieve. He told me that for him, dying would be like getting better.'

Dawn on the day after the battle on the River. A smell of baking bread from the villages. Cattle lowing, a woman calling her children. Fruitbats flickering over the reeds.

The River was rising fast, already lapping the date-palms where Hylas had hidden the day before. Echo perched in a tamarisk tree well back from the water's edge. Pirra sat beneath, watching little black fish darting in the shallows, where yesterday there had been dusty earth.

'Userref,' she said out loud. Then she said it again, and again, because he'd told her once that to speak the name of the dead is to help them live for ever.

Yesterday, she'd been shaken by the battle with the Crows and the horror of Alekto's death. Since then she'd slept, and dreamt of Userref at peace in the Place of Reeds. That had made her feel much better.

It was a relief, too, to have washed off the face-paint and changed into a simple knee-length tunic. Berenib hadn't minded about the state of her borrowed finery, and had been far more concerned about getting her clean.

Herihor and Rensi had just come to see her. The omens for the Flood were excellent, and Herihor was so relieved that he'd given Pirra a beautiful leather cuff for her forearm. Rensi said she should be flattered, as it was one of the few times that Herihor had ever given a gift to someone who was still alive.

Shortly afterwards, Meritamen had arrived. She and Kerasher had watched from the East Bank as the barbarians battled it out, and Alekto met her death, and Telamon brandished the dagger with a triumphant roar, before setting off for the coast. Then Meritamen had known that Pa-Sobek was rid of the Crows at last; and Kerasher had known that the decree of the Perao had been fulfilled.

'Although I'm sure that when Kerasher tells the Perao how it came about,' Meritamen had said drily, 'he will say that it was *Kerasher* who found the barbarians' dagger, not Hy-las.'

The Egyptian girl had seemed keen to atone for her past ruthlessness, and was so grateful to Hylas and Pirra for ridding her land of the Crows that she'd granted them safe-conduct to the coast, and had found a boat willing to take them. She'd also brought Pirra a gift, a beautiful little ivory comb with a horse carved on the back. Pirra accepted it with chilly reserve. She could not forget that Meritamen had been prepared to doom Userref's spirit in order to save her family.

Meritamen had a gift for Hylas, too: a new bronze knife in a splendid sheath of braided calfhide.

'You should give it to him yourself,' said Pirra. 'He's out in the desert with his lion, he'll be back soon.'

But the Egyptian girl flushed and shook her head. 'No, no,' she said hastily. 'Better if I don't see him again.' Her eyes filled. 'He would have died for you, Pirra,' she said wistfully. 'You are so lucky to have such a man.'

But he's not my man, thought Pirra. And I don't know if he ever will be.

Above her, Echo perched with beak agape and wings half-spread, keeping cool. She glanced at Pirra, but didn't fly down. Pirra guessed that the falcon was still wary of the new cuff.

Hylas came and sat beside her with his elbows on his knees. He'd tied his hair with a twist of grass, and he looked much more his old self. Pirra wanted him to put his arm around her, but he didn't. She was too proud to put her arm around him because she knew something was holding him back. She used to think it was her scar, but she didn't any more. It was something else. She wished she knew what.

She asked if he'd found Havoc, and he said yes, and told her about meeting Kem. But she could see from his face that he'd heard bad news.

'Rensi just got word from downriver,' he said. 'The Crows are making astonishing speed. With forty men at the oars and the current getting stronger all the time, they'll reach the Sea in a few days.'

'Well. That means they won't be lying in wait for us when we head north.'

'Oh no, they'll be long gone,' he said bitterly. 'Telamon will be eager to get back to Mycenae. Telamon the triumphant, returning with the dagger of Koronos!' He was scowling, clenching and unclenching his fists. 'I had it in my hand, Pirra! Now they've got it, and it's all to do again.'

Pirra saw the *wedjat* round his neck, with its fateful dent. She thought of the moment when he'd stepped out into the open with his chest bared to Telamon's arrow: for her. 'Do you regret that you threw it to him?' she said quietly.

'Of course not, he'd have killed you! But we're back

where we started – again. Sometimes I think I'll spend my whole life wandering, never returning to Lykonia, never finding Issi.'

Pirra was silent. For her, Lykonia and Issi were merely names. To Hylas, they were the place where he'd grown up, and the sister he'd known for longer than he'd known her.

'I can't bear not knowing what happened to her,' he said in a low voice. 'Worrying all the time. What if I never find out?'

There was nothing she could say to make him feel better, so she kept silent.

They watched a stripy kingfisher perch on a rock with a fish in its beak. It bashed the fish on the rock till it stopped wriggling, then gulped it down.

Pirra said, 'It wasn't for nothing, Hylas. If we hadn't come to Egypt, Userref's spirit would have been lost for ever, and Nebetku would be facing eternity without him.' She swallowed. 'While you were in the desert, I had a dream. I saw Userref and Nebetku in the Place of Reeds. They were both healthy and – so *happy*. What you did – swapping scrolls – it worked. Userref is there already, and soon Nebetku will be with him.'

Fiercely, she blinked back tears. Then she spoke the spell Rensi had taught her: *I have thrown off my tomb wrappings and am reborn like the lotus. The doors of the sky are opened for me. As a falcon I have flown up into the light, and my spirit is free.'*

'Be at peace, Userref,' she said in Akean. 'Until the River flows upstream and the raven turns white: be at peace.'

32

The next morning, they left Pa-Sobek and started north.

The boat Meritamen had found for them turned out to be Itineb's. With the *heb* over and the River rising fast, he and his brothers were heading home, and only too happy to take Hylas, Pirra *and* Havoc – particularly as Meritamen was paying them so well that they'd be returning to their village rich men.

Hylas was hugely relieved. It meant they could keep Pirra's last piece of Keftian gold to buy passage to Akea – *and* they didn't have to persuade a group of unknown Egyptians to take a lioness on board. 'We just need to keep her well fed,' he told Pirra. 'That way, she won't go after any cattle.'

'Or cats or dogs or children,' she added drily.

With the strengthening current, they made good speed. As Hylas watched the banks gliding past, it seemed that Egypt was slipping away behind him like a brilliantly coloured dream – or like tomb paintings sliding back into the darkness after the torch has passed on.

They slid past a sandbank where crocodiles basked in the Sun. Hylas thought of Alekto. Clearly, Pirra was thinking the same thing, because she turned to him, and her eyes were shadowed. 'I think her death was my doing.'

'What do you mean?'

'I asked Nebetku to write me a spell to bring ruin to its wearer. He wrote it in red ink, and I made a little crocodile out of wax. Then I wrapped the spell around it and put it in a pouch. When I was in the boat with Alekto, I tricked her into taking it off me.'

'But – that put you in danger too. When the boat was sinking, why didn't you tell her what it was? She'd have flung it overboard and you'd have been safe.'

She turned back to the River. 'Because I'd sworn to avenge Userref.'

Hylas looked at her. In her hawklike profile he saw the strength of her mother, the High Priestess of Keftiu.

'Telamon could have saved her,' she said. 'Instead he left her and went after you. But it was my spell that drew the crocodiles.'

Hylas regarded her with new respect. Kem was right. There were not many girls like Pirra.

He was jolted awake around midnight by a clamour on the bank. Havoc was gone, but Pirra was awake. Like him, she'd drawn her knife.

Together they listened to drums, shouts and the clash of weapons. It was coming from a large village a short distance from where Itineb and his brothers had moored for the night. Figures leapt in a blaze of torchlight, waving weapons at the sky.

'They're not fighting,' said Pirra. 'More like – trying to ward something off.'

'Look at the Moon,' muttered Hylas. It was a strange, dull red that he'd never seen before.

The boat tilted as Itineb jumped on board. 'Demons attacking the Moon,' he said in a low voice. 'The villagers are chasing them away. Look, it's working!' The rim of the Moon was glowing silver.

'Blood on the Moon means fighting to come,' added Itineb. 'I spoke to the village wisewoman. She said it won't be in Egypt, thank the gods, but far to the north.'

Hylas and Pirra exchanged glances. 'Akea,' they said.

With his stump, Itineb straightened his wig. 'I asked the wisewoman to read the Moon's markings. She said: *There is calamity in the Land of the North Wind. The rivers run with blood, and yet the people still drink from them – and the black-winged enemy casts a long shadow . . .'*

'The Crows,' said Pirra.

It seemed to Hylas that he saw a great bronze fist reaching out to seize Akea. Now that the Crows had the dagger, they were invincible. They wouldn't be content with Mycenae and Lykonia. They would go after Arkadia, too, and Messenia, where Issi was hiding.

They would want it all.

Towards dawn, he sat with Pirra in the prow, watching the dark River gliding past. Havoc sat between them. Hylas scratched one furry ear, and Pirra scratched the other. Hylas wanted to touch her fingers, but he hesitated and she noticed, and put her hands in her lap.

'I haven't yet thanked you for what you did,' she said after a while. 'I mean, offering yourself to Telamon . . .'

Hylas shifted and made a noise in his throat. He didn't want to be thanked.

Havoc rubbed her cheek against his calf, urging him to go on stroking. When he didn't, she rested her head on his knee and gazed up at him with big Moon-silvered eyes.

He knew he must answer the question that Pirra was too proud to ask. 'Pirra,' he began. 'It's not your scar that's keeping us apart. It never was – or that you're highborn and I'm not.' He touched his temple. 'The visions are getting worse.'

She looked at him. 'What do you mean, worse?'

'They're much clearer. And I – I see gods . . . I saw them after Telamon shot me. That's why I just stood there, when you were yelling at me to take cover.' He paused. 'What if next time it happens, I put *you* in danger? I mean, because I'm having a vision?'

Echo lit on to Pirra's shoulder. Distractedly, she touched the falcon's scaly foot. 'Here's what I think,' she said at last. 'When Telamon shot you, the gods let you live. If the *wedjat*'s thong had been a finger longer or a finger shorter, you'd be dead. But it wasn't, Hylas. The gods let you live. I think that's a good sign.'

He blew out a long breath. Then nodded slowly. 'Maybe.'

'Well it's good enough for me. No one knows what the future holds. But there's always hope.'

The girl had curled up and gone to sleep, but the boy remained awake. The she-lion sensed that he was still worried and unhappy, so she leant against him to cheer him up.

She was glad to see that he was finally growing some hairs on his chin: soon he would have a proper mane that went all the way round his face. The she-lion decided that from now on, she must give him plenty of licking and muzzle-rubs, to help it grow.

The Light was coming, and soon the Great Lion in the Up would turn fierce. The she-lion sat beside her boy, rumbling with the contentment that comes from a full belly, and feeling relieved that this floating pile of reeds no longer made her sick.

Earlier in the Dark, she'd gone hunting in the burning lands, and killed a buck. After eating till her belly was taut, she'd left the rest for the jackals and the spotted laughing dogs, who'd been slinking about, too scared to get any closer. That was good: dogs *should* be scared of lions.

The falcon was asleep, perched on the tree that grew from the floating reeds. As usual, she'd tucked one foot under her belly, and fallen asleep with one eye shut and one eye open. This was weird, but the she-lion was used to it. And she was glad that at last the falcon understood that she, too, belonged with the pride.

With a huge yawn, the she-lion rose to her feet and gave the boy a rasping lick on the jaw. He batted her away, so she play-batted him back. When he got up again, she gave him another lick, and he started making the yelping sounds that were his way of laughing. Then the girl woke up, the falcon flew down, and the whole pride was together.

This made the she-lion *extremely* happy. It was how things should be.

The Crocodile Tomb *is the fourth book in the story of Hylas and Pirra, which tells of their adventures in Akea, Keftiu and Egypt, and of their fight to vanquish the Crows. The last book in the series will be published in 2016.*

Author's Note

The *Crocodile Tomb* takes place three and a half thousand years ago, in what we call ancient Egypt. Hylas and Pirra aren't Egyptian, of course, they're from Ancient Greece. So I'll say a bit about them first, and then go on to Egypt.

Hylas and Pirra's World

We don't know much about Bronze Age Greece, as its people left so few written records, but we do know something about their astonishing cultures, which we call the Mycenaeans and the Minoans. (Hylas is Mycenaean, and Pirra is Minoan.)

It's thought that this was a world of scattered chieftaincies, separated by mountain ranges and forests, and that it was wetter and greener than today, with far more wild animals in both land and sea. Also, this was long before the Ancient Greeks ranged their gods into an orderly pantheon of Zeus, Hera, Hades, and so on. That's why the gods Hylas and Pirra worship have different names; they were the forerunners of the later lot.

To create the world of Hylas and Pirra, I've studied the archaeology of the Greek Bronze Age. To get an idea of peoples' beliefs, I've drawn on those of more recent peoples who still live in traditional ways, as I did in my Stone Age series, *Chronicles of Ancient Darkness*. And although most people in Hylas' time lived by farming or fishing, I think much of the knowledge and beliefs of the Stone Age hunter-gatherers would have survived into the Bronze Age, particularly among poorer people, such as Hylas himself.

Concerning **place names**, Akea (or Achaea, as it's often spelt) is the ancient name for mainland Greece, and Lykonia is my name for present-day Lakonia. I haven't changed the name Mycenae, as it's so well-known. And I've used the name 'Keftian' for the great Cretan civilization we call Minoan. (We don't know what they called themselves; depending on which book you read, their name may have been Keftians, or that may have been a name given to them by the ancient Egyptians.)

The **map** of the World of *Gods and Warriors* shows the world as Hylas and Pirra experience it, so it leaves out many places and islands that don't come into the story, and includes others that I made up, such as the Island of the Fin People and Thalakrea.

Ancient Egypt

If you're keen on Ancient Egypt, you might like to know that the story takes place at the start of what we call the New Kingdom, that is, the Eighteenth Dynasty, just after the Second Intermediate Period, when the Egyptians had rid themselves of the people called the Hyksos, who'd taken over the Nile delta. In the story, these are the foreigners from the east whom the Perao (Pharaoh) has ousted with the help of Koronos' bronze. (We don't know much about the Hyksos, which is why I'm being vague.)

Concerning Ancient Egyptian words and writing, unlike Hylas and Pirra's people, the Ancient Egyptians left *lots* of written records. I've tried to use real Ancient Egyptian names as much as I can, but there's a big BUT, which is actually pretty fascinating. Ancient Egyptian writing, which we call hieroglyphs (or the hieroglyphic script), didn't include vowels. They simply left them out. No 'a, e, i, o, u'. So in a sense, they wrote in a kind of ancient text-speak.

This means that archaeologists have to guess which vowels go where, or reconstruct words from later sources. For example, the Ancient Egyptian word for 'sun' was written 'r', and archaeologists think it was pronounced 're' (although in some books, you'll see it as 'ra'). And in the story, when Itineb tells Hylas about 'Shemu', he's using the Ancient Egyptian word for 'summer', which was written 'smw'.

You may be wondering why the Egyptian **gods** in the story have different names from those you might have read elsewhere. This is because I've used their Ancient Egyptian names, rather than those we commonly use today, which are derived from Greek versions. Thus:

Ausar: Osiris (green-faced god)
Anpu: Anubis (jackal-headed god)
Sekhmet: Sekhmet (lioness-headed goddess)
Heru: Horus (falcon-headed god)
Het-Heru: Hathor (cow-headed goddess)
Sobek: Sobek (crocodile-headed god)
Tjehuti: Thoth (ibis- or baboon-headed god)

A quick word on Ta-Mehi, the Great Green. Archae-ologists used to think this was Ancient Egyptians' word for the sea, but many now believe it refers to the Nile delta, and that's how I've used it in the story. Also, I've kept the name 'Egypt', even though it's derived from Greek, because it felt too artificial to change it.

For the **map** of Egypt, I've included *only* those places which are important to the story, because otherwise it would have been too cluttered. And Pa-Sobek in the story is only loosely based on present-day Kom Ombo, and I've moved it a bit further south.

I should also say something about **mummification**. Animals were mummified in enormous numbers in Egypt, but this was at a later period than the time in which the story is set. (It's in this later period that some of the most famous animal mummies were made, such as those in the animal catacombs at Saqqara.) However, animals had been mummified to a lesser extent for thousands of years before then, so I felt justified in inventing the Crocodile Tomb and its animal mummies.

To create the Egypt that Hylas and Pirra experience, I've drawn on my many visits to Egypt over the years. I've often been into the desert, and have seen many temple ruins, and climbed (or crawled) down lots of tombs, both royal and humble. Anyone who's done that will know how sweltering and claustrophobic it can get.

I also spent a day at the British Museum, learning how to write hieroglyphs in the authentic Ancient Egyptian way, using a rush pen and soot-based ink, on real papyrus (I needed a specially cut rush, as I'm left-handed!). My teacher was a calligrapher who's studied hieroglyphs. Watching this modern-day scribe at work, and hearing him talk, was fascinating. It's from him that I learnt about how to draw the bird symbols; and it's true that adding the beak is when you really feel you've created a bird.

The Nile has changed a lot from Hylas and Pirra's time. The papyrus has gone, and so have the crocodiles and hippos. And the river no longer floods, as it was dammed in the 20th century. But in places, there are still extensive reedbeds, which remain a paradise for birds, insects and reptiles. I've spent hours wandering through them at different times of the year. I've seen pied kingfishers, bee-eaters, glossy black ibis, egrets, all sorts of ducks, herons and other birds. My favourites are Hylas' 'purple moorhens', which are actually a kind of gallinule, like large purple chickens, with bright crimson legs and beaks.

As always, I am extremely grateful to Todd Whitelaw, Professor of Aegean Archaeology at the Institute of Archaeology, University College London, for providing me with pointers on various aspects of Bronze Age life. I also want to thank Paul Antonio for giving me some fascinating insights into how to write hieroglyphs during my day at the British Museum. And I want to thank my wonderful agent Peter Cox for his indefatigable commitment and support, and my hugely talented editor at Puffin Books, Ben Horslen, for his lively and imaginative response to the story of Hylas and Pirra.

MICHELLE PAVER, 2015

Discover more about the amazing world of

GODS AND WARRIORS

Q&A With Michelle Paver

What's it like being Echo?

Like all peregrine falcons, Echo has astonishing **eyesight.** She can spot a beetle on the ground when she's hovering high in the sky. And she can follow three moving objects at the same time, which helps when she's chasing a flock of pigeons and has to decide which one to attack. It's thought that she can see colours better than us, which is why when she looks at a crow, she sees it as bright green, purple and blue, as well as black. She can also sleep with one eye open, and turn her head right round, which is handy for spotting prey (or the dreaded ants!).

Her **ears** are better than ours at low frequencies, and she's better at detecting *where* a sound is coming from; and at picking one particular sound from a tangle of noises, which helps her find Pirra's voice in a crowd. Her ears can also detect **atmospheric pressure,** which means she knows how high she's flying, and when a storm's coming.

Her **nostrils** are on her beak, and she can smell quite well; although if she gets a cold, her nose runs. Her hard, arrow-like **tongue** can taste fairly well, which is why she spits out that stripy kingfisher in the Great Green (and pied kingfishers really do taste horrible, although I haven't tried them myself!).

Echo has a sense of **touch,** but not much in her feathers; her beak and feet are more sensitive, which is why Pirra gently strokes her toes. And her perception of **time** is different from ours: events we perceive as being incredibly fast appear much slower to her. That's why she sees damselflies 'lumbering past', when to us, they dart about in a blur.

Above all, Echo is *fast*. She's the fastest creature on the planet. She can fly horizontally at twice the speed a racehorse can gallop (that's about 110km or 70 miles per hour), and when she plunges in one of her great vertical dives, she reaches speeds of about 300km per hour (190 miles per hour). To fly so fast, she needs to hunt lots of prey. That's why she keeps getting distracted by all those birds in the Great Green!

In the story, both men like Kerasher and girls like Meritamen and Pirra wear eye make-up. In what other ways did Ancient Egyptians make themselves beautiful?

- Cleanliness was very important: they washed several times a day, chewed herbs or sacred salt (natron) to sweeten their breath, and used deodorant made of carob and incense.

- Eye make-up was widespread, and it also cut down the glare: both black kohl and green *wadju*, made from a ground-up green stone called malachite.

- Nails might be painted with henna (a red dye made from seed pods), and also the palms and soles of the feet. And lips might be glossed with fat mixed with red ochre or henna.

- People also used perfumes: mostly oil or fat scented with cinnamon, myrrh, lotus, frankincense, jasmine and other flowers or herbs, including mint and coriander.
- The men shaved, so that they never had beards, and both sexes might shave their legs and armpits, or remove the hair with wax.
- Some people kept their own hair and hennaed and plaited it, using setting lotion made of beeswax and tree resin. There's also an interesting recipe for hair ointment made of red ochre, myrtle, hippopotamus fat and gazelle dung. (I'm not sure if that's to remedy a scratchy scalp, make your hair shine, or both.) Another lotion to make the hair grow thicker involved boiling the bone of a dog, date kernels and donkey hoof in fat.
- And if you wanted to get your own back on someone, you boiled lotus leaves in oil, then smeared them on your enemy's head, to make their hair fall out!
- Many people shaved their scalps and wore wigs and/or hair extensions. The most expensive, like

Kerasher's, were of real human hair. The cheapest, like Itineb's were made of palm fibre, and must have been pretty scratchy.

- And as people got older, they tried to appear younger, in different ways:
  - To darken grey hair, they rubbed on ground-up gazelle horn and juniper berries.
  - To cure baldness, one recipe tells you to mix the fats of lion, hippopotamus, cat, snake, ibex and crocodile, then smear it on the head. Another recommends hedgehog bristles. (Presumably, you could grind those up and add them to the first recipe, for a sure-fire cure!)

What does the future hold for Hylas and Pirra in Book 5?

In *Warrior Bronze,* Hylas and Pirra – along with Echo and Havoc – find their way back to Akea, where Hylas' story began. But his homeland is caught in the clutches of the Crows, and Hylas himself is living on borrowed time, as his visions are getting stronger and more terrifying by the day.

Warrior Bronze is the final book in the Gods and Warriors series. Find out how Pirra copes in Hylas' harsh mountainous homeland, and whether Hylas ever discovers what happened to his long-lost sister Issi . . .